CONVERSATION WITH THE SEA

ALSO BY HUGO HAMILTON

Surrogate City

The Last Shot

The Love Test

Dublin Where the Palm Trees Grow

Headbanger

Sad Bastard

The Speckled People

The Sailor in the Wardrobe

Disguise

Head in the Fire

Every Single Minute

Dublin Palms

The Pages

Plays

The Speckled People (adaptation)

The Mariner

Every Single Minute (adaptation)

hugo

hamilton

conversation

with

the sea

HACHETTE
BOOKS
IRELAND

First published in 2025 by HACHETTE BOOKS IRELAND

1

Cover design: Ami Smithson.
Cover image: Detail from painting Overlap © Helen Glassford; helenglassford.co.uk

Cataloguing in Publication Data is available from the British Library

Hardback ISBN 978 1 39975 337 1
Trade paperback ISBN 978 1 39975 210 7
Ebook ISBN 978 1 39975 211 4

MIX
Paper | Supporting
responsible forestry
FSC
www.fsc.org   FSC® C104740

Typeset in Sabon LT Std by Bookends Publishing Services, Dublin
Printed and bound in Great Britain by Clays Ltd, Elcograf, S.p.A.

Hachette Books Ireland
8 Castlecourt Centre
Castleknock
Dublin 15, Ireland
A division of Hachette UK Ltd
Carmelite House, 50 Victoria Embankment, EC4Y 0DZ

www.hachettebooksireland.ie

Hugo Hamilton is the bestselling author of *The Speckled People*, a memoir of his German-Irish childhood in Dublin, growing up with his German mother and prohibited by his revolutionary Irish father from speaking English. It was translated into twenty languages and adapted for stage at the Gate Theatre. He has published ten novels, including *Dublin Palms* and *The Pages*, a collection of short stories, and a second memoir, *The Sailor in the Wardrobe*. His stories have appeared in the *New Yorker*. He has won numerous literary awards for his work, including the Prix Femina in France and the Bundesverdienstkreuz order of merit, awarded by the German state for his exploration of cultural diversity. Hamilton is a member of Aosdána and lives in Dublin.

One

In his journal he put down these words.

Arrived late afternoon. Blinded by the sun on the water. Could have driven right off the edge into the sea.

He parked the car and checked in at the guesthouse. His room overlooked the ocean. With the window left open he could hear the softly spoken waves unfolding on the shore. And once he had unpacked, he went straight out to walk along the beach. There was nobody in sight. He had the entire coastline to himself. Everything so still. So empty. So big and wide and for ever. The sunset lit up the sky in what he referred to in his journal as a red heart. A pumping red heart over a pumping red ocean. It turned the houses in the village behind him pink and the mountains a kind of burgundy. The cliffs on the far side of the bay became a red-bricked wall with ancient lines of distress left over from a time of great geological change.

This will make everything right, he said.

He could not be sure if he actually said it out loud or inside his head. His mouth was open and he found himself in conversation with the sea.

This will turn it all around, he said.

The sea listened.

He had come to stand at the edge of the world and look out across the Atlantic. Back to the place where they had spent their honeymoon together. She had now left him. She had moved out and taken their daughter Emilia with her to live in another part of Berlin and he had come to the west coast of Ireland to be healed by the vast distance that lay before his eyes. Things are a bit fucked-up back in Berlin right now, he said to the sea, and the sea replied in agreement that there was not much you could do now but listen to the waves and watch the colour of the sky changing and remember how to love the world.

I wish I could have persuaded her to come, he said. It might have brought us together again.

The sea looked sad.

He picked up a stick and wrote her name in the sand.

Katia.

The waves came in to erase her name even as he was spelling out the letters. That was the nature of the sea, to sweep everything aside and leave the sand clear and untouched for the next day. He asked if the sea could remember when they were on their honeymoon standing in this exact place in the copper sunlight and she took off her shoes and said the water was icy. He said to the sea, as if the sea had no memory, that she held her dress in her hand and said the sand was a piece of her childhood coming up through her feet. Her smile came ashore and the waves were up to her knees, do you remember that?

The sea remembered everything.

We know you, the sea said. Lukas. Lukas Dorn from Berlin. You haven't changed a bit. Big smile. Eyes full of trust. Navy overshirt with a journal in the right-hand pocket.

That's me. He laughed.

Luki.

He heard the sea using his family nickname, the name his mother gave him. His love name. What Katia used to call him in her phone messages, in whispers, in cries. The sea spoke to him as a friend he had known a long time ago and it was no time at all because the sea had been waiting for him to come back. The sea continued being the sea, not any older than it was before, living in a timeless time, while he lived in a time that was curtailed by time and everything was ultimately converted into memory. He had come to stand inside his own memory, watching the waves polishing a couple of pebbles, delivering them right up to his feet and taking them back again.

He turned and walked up to the village to get something to eat. He went into one of the pubs and found a round table where he sat down and was given a menu. The food was basic. He had fish and chips. He had a pint of Guinness and looked around to find that nothing had changed.

Everything was the same.

The same barman. The same faces at the bar. The same joke behind the bar that he could never remember. The same photograph on the wall of a turf boat making its way across the bay with brown sails. The same round table where he had sat with her back then and where he sat now by himself beneath the same old map with the names of all the places where they walked together. An ordnance survey map with the long beach where they stood kissing each other as the sun went down and the mountains were so sharply defined against the sky you could have cut yourself.

The musicians came in and took up a table reserved for them in the corner. The first squeak of the accordion. The pluck of fiddle strings. A short drumroll that sounded like it would be followed by a circus act. And once the musicians got into full swing, he watched them playing their high-speed tunes with a force that seemed so effortlessly authentic.

The woman who played the accordion had pink fingernails. Pink fingernails on black buttons, he wanted to tell Katia, if only she still wanted to know. He wanted to let her know it was a black-button accordion with golden sound vents and pink fingernails tapping the notes out like an urgent message to the heart. He wanted to let her know that nothing had changed. He was sitting at the same round table underneath the map of the island and the sea was asking for her.

It was late by the time he left the pub and so dark on his way back to the guesthouse he could hardly see a thing. His eyes were unable to adjust to the night. The stars made him stagger. He had no sense of direction other than the sound of the sea and he made his way slowly along the path with the light of his phone illuminating the ground.

He came face to face with a silent horse. The horse stood with its head leaning over a wall, watching him approaching step by step with the blue light showing the way. The horse waited until he was right up close and reared its head up at the very last minute when it was clear that he was not familiar. And it was only then that he jumped back, when he saw that the horse was not part of the wall but a living thing with one big glistening eye looking down at him. Nostrils flaring as they did in paintings of horses. They both took fright at once. Invisible hoofs galloping away through the night. A man with a phone in his hand and a translucent face.

His appearance on a sightless summer night full of memory with the stars out and the surf crashing on the beach frightened the horse and frightened him in turn. He was frightened by what frightened the horse. Something inside him, something he brought with him to this quiet place that must have caused the horse to panic, leaving him behind on the path like an apparition, he wrote in his journal.

The horse was gifted with subconscious sight. It had the ability to reach inside his head and see all those disturbing facts he carried in his memory. All the noise of the city and all the fucked-up things in his thoughts made the horse seek the shelter of darkness. This sensitive creature could not only forecast hurricanes and earthquakes and bog fires underground, it knew the inside of a man's head. His life story. His emotions. Sorrow. Joy. Love. Doubt. Guilt. The horse had access to parts of his mind that he could not even reveal to himself. All the ongoing uncertainties, the scary things, the stuff you kept to yourself and couldn't say.

It was not the arrival of a stranger on the path, not the fraudulent blue light of a mobile phone acutely shining upwards into that big horse-shocked eye but a hunch, a fact, a hidden piece of information in the backroom of his mind that became so alarming.

He heard a snort some distance away. He heard the sound of a hoof stamping on rock. The horse was observing him from that infinite darkness as he continued making his way back to the guesthouse. He saw the headlights of a car pointing into the sky, sweeping across the coast. The stone walls began to move. His shadow creeping along the path. And in his sleep, he heard the waves coming up to the foot of the bed.

Two

At breakfast the following morning, he laid his journal out on the table. He removed the strap that kept it closed and took up the pen clamped inside to write down how glad he was to be in such a quiet place, looking out the window at the sea.

The woman of the house brought a pot of tea and said it looked like a great day for sightseeing.

You're not a surfer, are you?

No, I'm not a surfer, he said.

They had a lot of surfers coming to the beach now, she said. It's popular with surfers from all over the world. Some of them wear Bermuda shorts over their wetsuits. They go up to the pub in their bare feet, so I'm told.

She laughed and he smiled back.

Smell of cooked breakfast, he wrote. Tea. Toast. Brown bread. Four golden envelopes of butter. Marmalade. Noise of plates and spoons.

The woman of the house came back at one point to ask if he wanted more homemade brown bread and he said it was the best homemade bread in the world, but he had plenty right now, thanks. He had just covered a slice with a thin film of marmalade and was about to bring it to his mouth while the woman of the house stood by watching him. He hesitated and put the slice of home-made brown bread back on his plate.

She picked up an empty plate and casually placed her hand on his shoulder in a manner that was both intrusive and kind-hearted at the same time. He found himself being gently pinned down in his chair with a physical intimacy that almost brought him to tears. She might as well have been his mother, waiting until he finished the slice of bread in front of him. She left her hand subconsciously resting on his shoulder and began telling him how during the winter, this winter gone by, she said, a storm had lifted the sand from one end of the beach and delivered it right on top of the house.

He twisted his head around to acknowledge that information with a look of surprise.

Wow, he said.

Wow, indeed.

She described waking up one morning to find the house entombed. That's the only word for it, she said. Entombed. We were like the pharaohs. We could not see out the windows, everything was dark. We couldn't open the front door. I swear to God, we were trapped inside – they might have found us mummified in a few hundred years. We had to get out through the kitchen window at the back. My husband spent weeks carrying the sand back to the beach with the help of some of the locals, you'd think he was an archaeologist.

He saw her husband passing by outside with a bucket.

Other guests came in for breakfast. They were obviously surfers, in bare feet. A man wearing chequered shorts. His partner had 'Everything Is Possible' printed across her chest and her eyes were remarkably blue, aquamarine.

The woman of the house took her hand off his shoulder and tapped it twice in a gesture of conclusion. Adding that the sand covering the house was probably one of those weather events they have been getting more of in recent years.

She walked over to ask the surfers what they wished to have for breakfast and told them it might be safer, if you don't mind, to keep the shoes on around the house because of the boiling hot tea. God forbid if something spilled on those lovely feet.

Lads, she called them. As if there was no gender distinction in her house.

The bread on his plate had vanished. He must have eaten it without awareness. He turned to his journal once more and made a quick note – weather event. House entombed. Archaeological dig.

It was as though his mind would fall apart if he didn't lay out the facts in contemporaneous order. His journal had become his only companion. He would have liked to tell Katia about the sand covering the house like a mausoleum. And the sand on the floor in the hallway like sugar crunching under his shoes. And the woman of the house telling the surfers off for coming to breakfast in their bare feet. But Katia was not his first receiver any more. He was no longer reporting to anyone but his journal.

He made a note about the woman of the house putting her hand on his shoulder. Woman of the house, he wrote, is quite motherly. Dressed more like a woman going out for the evening. Blue cardigan. White blouse with the collar turned up. Silk scarf tucked in at the front. Light fragrance. Possibly lily-of-the-valley. Tilts her head to the right when she smiles. Speaks with the commanding voice of a schoolteacher.

And while he was making these notes, certain that she was unable to read German, she seemed to suspect that he was writing about her. After delivering the full breakfast to the surfers, looking down to make sure she didn't step on any toes and saying, Mind, the plates are hot, she passed by his table again and stopped to glance over his shoulder.

Don't forget to mention the brown bread, she said.

Bread, he said.

Five stars, she added, with a laugh. Briefly touching his writing arm before going back out to the kitchen.

He drew five stars on the next page, just in case she came back to check.

When he was going out walking later on, he stopped in the hallway to hang up his key. On the hook with number nine written underneath. There was a small desk in the hallway with a bell and a hand-sanitising dispenser. Also, a stand of postcards with places worth visiting on the island, such as the beach where he and Katia had once stood with the sun going down. Beside the postcards was an honesty box. The time of postcards was gone since people sent their own pictures on their phones, more often of themselves with the sun going down.

On the wall behind the desk, he saw the same ordnance survey map that was hanging in the pub, showing the places identified in the postcards.

And just inside the front door, there was a large portrait of a German writer who had once stayed at the guesthouse, way back in the last century. The writer wore a black beret and had a cigarette dangling from his lips. The beret gave him the appearance of a revolutionary figure, standing in the middle of the road at a time when there was no traffic. An outmoded sort of guerrilla intellectual.

The writer had published a famous book of travel essays, which was like series of postcards sent home. He could remember reading those essays about the writer and his family arriving on the island in a pre-television age when the place was a paradise outside time. When life was like a postcard and the bus to Westport was full of emigrants leaving every Friday and the bus driver had to wait with the engine running for the last embraces before he could finally drive off. There was a passage in the book that he loved, about the island doctor going out in a storm in September to deliver a baby and his wife anxiously tracing the route with a red fingernail along the same map of the island in their home, and the doctor hooting his horn coming back through the village to let everybody know it was a boy.

And just when he was about to go out, the woman of the house came in the front door with a small bunch of wildflowers. She smiled and stood blocking his way as though she wanted to know what brought him to the island, apart from coming to see if the scenic beauty of the place was still the same as it was in the last century when the German writer with the revolutionary beret was there.

When he didn't volunteer anything about himself, she asked him if he would like a scone to take with him. He thanked her and said he had one of those protein bars, that would do him for the day.

She examined his facial expressions to explain the unanswered questions that lay behind his eyes. His inside face. An enigma to be unscrambled. A man who had come to the West of Ireland to be alone with his thoughts. Issues that could not be shared in bits of friendly chat with the woman of the house. He had an open face. A smile full of patient acquiescence. She could see that he might be carrying around some tragic interior life. A man who was missing something.

She had taken up a commanding position at the door, so he ended up telling her that he had been to visit the island before with his wife, on their honeymoon. They had a daughter now who was sixteen years of age, but they couldn't come because they were booked on a school trip to Madrid to see the art galleries. His wife was an art teacher and the woman of the house said, Oh, that's a shame they were not able to be here with you.

Busy schedule, he said.

And you came alone.

She waited for him to reply.

He could hardly tell her that his marriage was fucked, basically. That his wife had left him to pursue her career as an artist. She needed total freedom. The reckless, unrestrained optimism that was required to follow her ideas. He was getting in the way of her creativity with his hardcore vision of the world, to the point where she felt the beauty was gone out of their marriage. Her mind surging forward and his mind lurching back into the past. He was out there in the West of Ireland longing for the woman she once was, looking for a place with an old tree where they once stopped on their honeymoon. Where they parked the camper van they were travelling in and she wanted to sit under the tree in the rain.

Telling the woman of the house that he was looking for a tree was not going to reduce her concern for his mental well-being. Nor could he tell her that the break-up of his marriage coincided with a whole lot of other fucked-up things that were going on in the world right now and reminded him of all the fucked-up things that went on in history. There was no point in telling her, as he would have told his wife after dinner when he was offering her a cup of mint tea and a square of chocolate, that the world is not in great shape. His father spent his entire life coming to terms with the past and his daughter was having to come to terms with the future. And his wife was going around with paint on her hands.

They might be able to join me later, he said, as though that was the password required to get out the door.

Good for them.

Hopefully, he added, like a missing word.

He even gave the woman of the house their names – Katia and Emilia – just to authenticate his story and make it sound like they were still part of his life. That was the only way of getting her to step aside and let him out. Putting her mind at rest about him coming to a place like this alone with such dangerous beauty all around, full of emptiness and cliffs and deserted beaches, a bog where you could disappear and not be seen again, silence that he was not used to coming from a city like Berlin, with nothing in his pocket but an old energy bar and his journal.

Three

He walked up through the village past the pub and saw the horse being led into a horsebox by an old man and a young boy. The boy was inside pulling on the reins while the old man was encouraging, occasionally pushing from behind with a stick. The horse did not want to go. No matter how much the boy pulled on the reins, and the old man bribed the horse with sugar cubes that he carried in his pocket, it refused to move. The hoofs could be heard knocking on the wooden gangplank but then it reversed again, coming right back onto the road and turning away towards the sea. The old man, perhaps he was the boy's grandfather, then had to steer the horse around in circles before they could try afresh.

People had come to watch, mostly children. There were two mothers with their buggies, joined later by a future mother who arrived on a bike. She wore black leggings and a red top that proudly revealed her belly with the navel exposed, as though she had become suddenly pregnant and hadn't time to change. The afternoon was bright and one of the children bore an expression of distate, like it knew exactly how the horse felt being asked to go to bed when everybody else was still up. The mothers, present and future, spoke about the horse like a disobedient child refusing to be told what to do.

He became a spectator, watching the old man putting a blindfold over the horse's eyes. At that point, the horse had no idea where it might be taken to and refused to move in any direction. The old man put his arm around the horse's neck like a friend and spoke to it gently, offering a reward for cooperating, nothing bad was going to happen, no such thing.

At the next attempt to lure the horse up the slope, it suddenly bolted. The boy lost hold of the reins. The horse turned in circles trying to get the blindfold off and the clatter of hoofs on the road frightened the children. Mothers, present and future, backed away, reversing the buggies off the road. The children were told to stand back. In a moment of panic, the horse ran along the road towards the pub with the fish and chips. It crashed into the entrance of the pub and then turned around to seek a different route. The nostrils were flaring and the hoofs were making a tap-dancing noise on the road, so he heard a mother say to her children.

For a moment, it looked as though the blind horse was taking another run at the horsebox, but then it collided with a parked car and went skidding on the road. It tumbled over on its side with legs in the air, trying to run upside down. Belly up to the sky like a large insect not used to gravity, unable to get upright again.

The old man and the boy tried to get a hold of the reins, but the horse finally managed to stand up and get away with the reins slithering along the road, this time with the blindfold half off, enough to be able to make sure it didn't go into the horsebox by mistake.

Look, the horse is bleeding, he heard one of the boys saying to his mother.

There was a cut on the horse's neck that looked like a fresh bite taken out of a grey cake. Maybe a chunk of flesh was now attached to the tail end of the parked car. Whatever it was that had spooked the horse now sent it running away in the direction of the sea. A dog, normally accustomed to chasing cars, began to try and bite one of the hind legs. A sheep and lamb lying on the road jumped up and danced out of the way in black shoes. The boy was ahead of his grandfather as they ran after it. Some of the children joined in and a mother could be heard shouting after them not to go near an animal that was injured.

The horse had already reached the strand with a group of people in pursuit, including the husband of the woman who ran the guesthouse, dropping his bucket and leaving a small half-formed sandcastle outside the door.

On the shore, the surfers stood at the edge of the water some distance to the left, preparing to go out onto the waves as the horse went running towards them. The gap between those in pursuit had opened and it looked, from where he was standing, that the ratio would never be narrowed, the horse would always be ahead, galloping and splashing along the firm sand at the edge of the water. The old man was waving at the surfers to turn the horse around. They seemed to understand the message like a voiceless language of coastal signals. They picked up their surfboards like warrior shields and stood in a line waiting.

The frightened horse, as he would later describe it in his journal, came to a stop when it was confronted by this battalion of black figures from the deep.

The horse began to walk into the waves, splashing with one hoof in the tide, nuzzling at the waves and the white foam that seemed to come from its mouth and spread around its feet. Maybe it wanted to wash off the blood on its flank and shake the pain out of its neck. The surfers, as far as he could see from that distance, tried to surround the horse but it turned and ran back along the shore in the opposite direction, towards the spot where he had once stood with Katia in a copper glow with the sun setting.

He continued watching this emergency unfolding on the beach and it seemed, if you abolished the element of time, that everything in the world was related in some personal way to his own life. The past and the present seemed to overlap and the horse came running back to where he once stood with Katia at the edge of the ocean.

The surfers with their warrior shields joined the men and boys who had now prevented the horse from running anywhere past the point where he and Katia stood with the pumping red heart. Their spontaneous plan was to close in on the horse and trap it between land and sea. Between life and death, in other words. The horse had nowhere to turn, so it made the reckless decision to run out into the sea and become part of the ocean, one more grey wave going against the tide.

At that point, the boy who had earlier been helping the old man to pull the horse into the horsebox had managed to regain control of the reins. The horse was so determined to escape whatever grief was lodged in its head that it began to pull the boy out to sea with him. The old man was up to his waist in the waves. The boy and the reins out of reach. Only the horse's head above the water line with enlarged nostrils and small horse-frightened eyes, a red scarf of blood, bared teeth and white foam around the mouth.

Along with the other men on the shore, the old man was shouting at the boy to let go of the reins but the sound of the surf may have obscured their voices and made the boy think he was doing the right thing. The boy continued holding on, so it looked as though the horse and the boy were doomed to drown together. They had, it seemed to me, he later wrote, gone onto the list of drowned names down through the history of this quiet and dangerous place, some recovered, some not, some unknown and still missing, some turned into tragic ballads.

Come under, the sea was calling. Come under and be rescued from life.

The horse was consigned to departure with pointed ears turned back, while the sea kept calling from the deep and the boy rider was being tossed around as though he could not live without the horse.

The people on the shore seemed helpless. There was no reasoning with the sea and they had no way of averting what was happening before their eyes. Until the surfers dropped their shields and ran into the waves. They were no longer dealing with a horse but a super wave to be conquered. They swam out and took the reins off the boy. One of them carried the boy back to the shore and laid him on the sand, but the boy instantly got up again to run after the horse, with his grandfather holding him back.

The other surfers continued swimming after the horse, getting into a tug of war with the waves as the sea was calling the horse down into the deep.

Come under. Come down and be saved. Be free, the sea kept saying to the horse with its head still above the waves and teeth shaped in a terrified grin. The surfers were pulling the reins and the reins seemed to get longer and longer until the horse appeared to be going to join the countless deep.

That vast, sentient mass of water, he wrote in his journal, heaving and pulling. A deep, underwater state of being containing all the emotions of the world. All that history of migration and longing, all those sea crossings and parted lovers and boats setting out for a new start and communication cables lying on the floor of the ocean. An oceanic life force calling the horse to be free of the reins. Be drowned. Be saved. Come down and join us in the deep green deep.

Two of the surfers had managed in the meantime to swim out beyond the horse and whatever they said overruled the sea with their imperial skills. They turned the horse back in the direction of trusted land, coaching it to join the cult of survival. They rode the incoming waves towards the shore, swimming and surfing and surviving, until the horse finally walked out of the water like a spent wave, exhausted.

The sea was full of anger now, squally and wishing a storm. The boy was holding on to the reins once more and the old man was feeding the horse sugar cubes. The husband of the woman of the house was feeling its legs to make sure nothing was broken. The surfers stood in a cluster talking about great waves they had mastered in scenic locations around the world, legendary curlers with star ratings, but none of them came close to the horse. They were the heroes of the hour. Like some guardians of nature, they had not only rescued the boy and the horse from drowning but also taken part in some crusading act to save the planet.

People came out of their houses. They were gathered in small groups talking about the event. He heard them say the vet had been called to administer a tranquilliser along with a course of antibiotics to prevent sepsis. They were asking what madness had taken hold of the horse that made it so dangerously agitated? The grey horse, normally so tranquil and stationary, standing in a field in the rain, staring ahead like it was part of the landscape, now driven by some extraordinary premonition, perhaps, some coming harm that made it want to escape the earth.

Four

He spent the day out on the bog. The road was dancing with insects and he heard the sound of an accordion. A phantom note coming across the bog, full of longing. It was carried over the stone walls and fields. It hummed inside red fuchsia hedges. A sustained musical breath that expanded across the sea and went overland on Autobahns and railway lines along the continental landmass to Berlin.

The sound of the accordion turned out to be a motorbike coming along the road. An older couple, passing through the strong sunlight. The woman on the back of the bike raised her hand to wave at him and it was too late to wave back by the time they were gone by.

Perhaps he was being corrupted by the beauty of the place. He was in hock to a dream. Walking through a view that was not only full of personal memory and vivid recollections of Katia with red cheeks in the wind, but a landscape that was so scenic, so silent, so mythological, it seemed to have become aware of its own beauty.

Surrounded by that profound silence on the bog, he tried to explain what it was that had driven Katia away. What made her withdraw her smile? What made her afraid of love? With no place of safety in their relationship? Some general anxiety inside him that made him impossible to live with. A sense of global foreboding he carried inside and had now attached itself to the horse on this remote island.

He recalled an event in Berlin that seemed to forecast all this inevitable dissolution. An incident in an underground station that felt to him like a key moment from which everything sprang into motion. It happened some time before their separation, so it now seemed like some weird prophecy of what was coming.

He remembered standing on the platform, seeing a man asking for money. The man going from person to person on the platform spoke with an accent from elsewhere. Tall and thin, wearing a pink jacket that must have been given to him by some charity, it was too small. A furry jacket, zipped up at the front with his chest bare underneath. Canvas slippers with the heels turned down, no socks.

He recalled how he was on his way to the dental hygienist at the time and reached into his pocket to give the man in the furry pink jacket some coins, enough to buy a kebab.

The man went on to approach a couple standing some metres away who ignored him. They were in the middle of a conversation and didn't want to be disturbed. They went back to staring into each other's eyes and the man in the pink bomber jacket lost it. He walked to the edge of the platform and began to shout.

You don't give a shit, do you?

The couple moved away.

Here, watch this, you people, the man said, then turned and jumped down onto the tracks. The electronic screen over the platform showed the train was due in one minute.

The reason this event continued to pursue him, as he stood on a bog full of brown emptiness on the outer edge of Europe, was not so much the horror of the moment in the station but the familiar feeling of powerlessness. The inability to stop what was coming. Helpless in the station and helpless in his own life and helpless in the terms of everything else that was going on in the world.

This was exactly the kind of situation his father had warned him and his older brother Peter about from a very early age, the duty of care to fellow human beings. His father was a history professor with special interest in the erasure of memory. He could recall his father talking about the innocent bystander. People who stood by and failed to intervene. People pretending to be blind, he could still hear his father say over breakfast in his daily speeches before they went to school. Drilling the faculty of empathy into them as if it was something each child had to learn, like the alphabet.

His mother had a similar terror of what you might be forced to witness. Don't gawk, she always said when they passed by the scene of an accident. While people in other cars slowed down to have a good look, she turned away. And whenever they came back from a journey, she would walk in the door and say, Thank God nothing happened and thank God we didn't see anything awful either.

The people on the platform were waiting in a passive state for what was coming next. They could already hear the train rumbling in the tunnel. They felt the wind-suck around their legs, ruffling hair, lifting the flaps of jackets.

Wait till you see, the man in the furry pink jacket continued shouting. Just watch.

You people.

The man turned his back to the oncoming train and crossed his arms, waiting for the end.

What made him like this? he wondered. Was something done to him? Drink? Drugs? Had he come from a war zone? The city was full of refugees.

He's off his head, somebody muttered. Others were telling him to get the hell out of there, for God's sake, are you insane? In an effort to help the man on the tracks, he reached out his hand, but found himself being pulled back by the elbow and told, He might drag you down with him.

Human incident, he wrote in his journal afterwards. That's what they announce over the speakers when there is no other technical explanation.

The man in the furry jacket had lost one of his shoes. He was slipping his bare foot back in as though he wanted to be ready for what was coming. The train had already reached the station. People watched in horror. Some turned away so they didn't have to witness it. Others continued staring like captive spectators with the screech of wheels approaching, waiting for the inevitable click of bones and soft tissue. As the train came speeding into the station, he saw the motionless expression on the driver's face. And just before that moment of blood and guts, just before the worst came to the worst, the man on the tracks jumped up with his backside onto the platform, swinging his legs out of the way at the last minute with both shoes on.

Somebody called him a suicide artist. A con man. They felt duped. Their compassion had been taken for a ride. A theatrical performance to extract sympathy. Somebody made the gesture of a needle going into his arm.

The doors opened. People got off and people got on. Life continued on schedule as the train pulled out of the station and the man in the furry pink jacket turned up in the same carriage with his hand out. Some of the passengers gave him money, others kept looking at their phones or staring up at the info screen advertising the latest movies, bits of celebrity gossip.

He had taken the incident to heart. It was added to all the other things he kept in his journal, things that mattered in his life as a man, a father, a son, a lover, a traveller on a journey to find where he belongs. It seemed to contain a prediction. Like predictions only become predictions when the thing actually happens and you're looking back. It foretold, in hindsight, all the shit that had now arrived along with the break-up of his marriage. As though it was all leading to the end of something, the end of nature, the end of everything. The big wedding of the world that brought them together in a moment of great euphoria after the Berlin Wall came down was now over. They were in their late forties and already in the aftermath, that disarray of chairs and tables and knocked over wine glasses. All that East–West, Berlin cool, met in a club, post-Wall couple, art and food and music and low rent, love at every sight, honeymoon for life, now falling apart.

Five

On the way back, he was blinded by the sunlight. The sea at the end of the road was full of glitz and bling. He wore no cap and no sunglasses and the view was misleading. What he thought were dolphins might have been surfers. What he thought were surfers might have been bits of seaweed. White sheets on a line billowing like sailboats on the breeze. A trawler making its way back into the harbour with a tattered flag of seagulls.

He came to a small bridge and stood mindlessly staring at a stream, watching the time going by in cubic litres of brown bog water, when he felt a buzzing on his phone. A photo received from his daughter.

He turned away to shade the screen from the sun so that he could examine it. It showed the famous *Guernica* painting at the Reine Sofia Gallery in Madrid. While most of the visitors were looking at the painting, two students stood facing the camera, unfurling a banner in protest. A cloth poster, made from a white bedsheet, scrawled with paint the colour of blood.

The canvas covered an entire wall with a row of students in front. A girl with a phone in her back pocket. A boy leaning his arm on the shoulder of another boy.

Katia was in the shot, pointing at *Guernica*.

The gallery had been the site of public demonstrations against war in the past and *Guernica* now had a security guard positioned at each end of the painting, scanning visitors closely at all times. Making sure nobody crossed the white rope that cordoned visitors off from the actual artwork. It was such a large work, better seen at a distance of four metres at least, from behind the white rope. The horror depicted in the painting was no better up close.

He had only seen *Guernica* in photographs himself. The painting was done in black and white, but the viewer remembered it in colour. He felt he had missed something by not seeing it in person, a cultural duty he had failed to fulfil so far. He was not in a position to speak about *Guernica* unless he had seen *Guernica*.

Looking down at the photo sent by his daughter, he zoomed in on her mother. She was seen from behind wearing a light green jacket he had never noticed before. The sleeves were rolled up as though it was bought for somebody bigger than her. Standing with her arm up and her thin wrist emerging from the rolled-up sleeve, it seemed to him that she was pointing at the horse.

Her hand became part of the painting, telling the students most probably to focus on the expression of pain and fear in the horse's eyes. It was a grey horse, not unlike the horse that had run into the sea, a large black and white canvas depicting the chaos of war. The painting had come to life and the horse was seen under a light bulb, its long neck stretching up from the terror of nocturnal bombing. The eyes vertical and the nostrils flared. Mouth wide open in the agony of death with three upper teeth and four lower teeth at unnatural angles. The tongue shaped like the tip of a screaming spear. The horse was like a cartoon image, he later wrote in his journal, increasing the horror through comic exaggeration. The horse was trapped by the artist in cruel perpetuity between life and death, allowing the viewers behind the white rope to experience the full horror of *Guernica*.

When he managed to get Emilia on the phone, he first had to explain to his daughter that the sound of water flowing by was a stream. A stream coming down from the mountain, he said, going all the way into the sea. He asked her if she would like to come and join him out there on the island.

For what?

Well, he said, there's the sea and the mountains. And bogs full of silence.

Emilia laughed.

You could take up surfing.

She laughed again.

She told him that her mother had since been called in front of a school tribunal after the trip to Madrid. The cloth poster had been carried into the gallery surreptitiously by one of her students. Another student had taken the photo. The image of the unfurled poster had been disseminated over social media with the name of the school mentioned.

His daughter told him that her mother had drawn the attention of the students to what *Guernica* was saying about the present. Pointing at the horse, she said, her mother commented that it was a warning from the past. This had been reported to the tribunal by one of the students. It placed her mother in a precarious position because her words were seen as a clear link to the unfurled banner. Her job was on the line. She had been suspended along with the two students who had held up the bloodied sheet, as well as the student who had taken the photo and released it on various social media platforms.

Why didn't she tell me?

I'm telling you, his daughter said.

The school board took issue with such an overt connection being made between past and present. Pointing the finger at the horse with her green sleeve rolled up in the same photograph with a bloodied banner made her a participant in the protest. There was no excuse for not knowing what was happening behind her. It was assumed that she had put the students up to it.

Her mother, his daughter said, had been questioned about her attitude to the past. Was she aware how offended the present was at being compared to the past? It was outrageous to link history with what was happening in recent times, one member of the school board said in a raised voice. Her mother had to defend her position and let the tribunal know it was not her intention to diminish the past. That would never have crossed her mind, not for one instant. The number of screaming horses alone bore no comparison.

The school board had, apart from the new sports hall, invested heavily over the years in history management, to the point that it was seen as one of the top schools in Berlin. The unfurled banner had caused serious reputational damage. It was not, her mother was told, what parents would expect. The board of management accepted her remorse and guilt over the incident at the Reine Sofia Gallery in Madrid, but the case was now going to arbitration.

Is she seeing her therapist? he asked.

She's OK, Emilia said.

The guy with the ponytail?

No, she said. It's a woman. She does all these breathing techniques and humming.

This will all blow over soon, he told his daughter to say to her mother, and it was unclear if that was referring to the break-up or the trouble with *Guernica*.

His daughter had become an envoy between him and her mother. Everything he said to her might as well have been said to her mother. It could easily have been her mother who was talking to him on the phone while he stood beside all that brown bog water flowing by. They looked so alike, same voice, same hair, same eyes. That smile full of inner life. Like it was always her birthday and there was something funny, some deep, untroubled, inviting sense of irony inside her head that made people want to go right over and talk to her.

Sometimes they borrowed clothes from each other and he noticed that she had begun wearing a loosely woven russet cardigan that he had bought her mother.

When he got off the phone with his daughter, he sent her mother a message, saying he had seen the photo and it was ridiculous to make an art teacher responsible for preventing the truth from coming out. He knew exactly what he would say to those people on the tribunal if he got the chance. If I were you, he wanted to say to her, but he was not her and she was not him. They were gone well past that time of speaking for each other with the same mind.

Katia didn't need him telling her how to defend herself. He turned his message into an expression of support and encouragement. He offered to talk to her. He was available any time to discuss a strategy. He received an emoji of two praying hands in return.

He put the phone into his pocket and made his way down to the sea. The sound of the accordion followed him like a persistent lament and the couple on the motorbike passed him by on their way back. A couple of crows in a tree made a lot of noise with dissenting hearts. A dog came out to sniff at him as he passed by a farmyard.

The sun was so bright on the water it made his eyes water. He heard the bark of a seal. The shriek of a heron. A flock of turnstones flew across the water in a wide circle only to come back to where they had started on the shore.

From the blinding sea, the surfers emerged like mythical figures on the waves, standing up and surfing and sinking down. Again and again, they carried out these small, heroic acts of survival. They stood on top of the breakers in black costumes, like immortal beings defying all earthly dimensions. They seemed to carry no sorrow, no suffering, only that repeated assertion of life. The sport of self-affirmation was what he later called it in his journal, full of wonderful human balancing acts. Like the natural world had been found out and the sea had become a great spectacle of submission.

Six

He found it hard to sleep. With the sound of the waves coming up to his feet, he felt he might surrender to unsafety and become part of the sea. He was afraid for the horse and afraid for Katia and afraid for *Guernica* and lots of other unspecified things. His journal lay open on his lap and he wrote how he felt responsible for the break-up of his marriage. His obsession with the past must have gradually driven her away. An incongruous memory. At the most inappropriate moments, he would remember seeing his mother in hospital and being unable to let that go. How different she had looked in the bed as he stood there with his older brother and his father, unable to recognise her until she spoke with a frail voice and took his hand.

He had his headphones on to calm his mind with music. It released him from the constant duty of explanation. A track from a playlist he could trust, beginning with a set of atmospheric notes backed up by the sound of wind blowing across empty terrain. Choral voices, perhaps female, perhaps no gender at all, possibly constructed from non-human recordings. Beings with no faces moving across the beach where nobody stood now and the sea was full of harm.

When the track came to an end, he suddenly remembered Katia accusing him of undermining her confidence. Moments when she glared at him for making a comment, or failing to comment, on her art. The time he bought her a set of expensive paintbrushes when the ones she already had were perfectly good, and she said he was trying to earn the right to direct her artistic vision. Encouraging her with a heavy hand. Gently proposing improvements she hadn't asked for. She was not looking for the kind of historical depth he was suggesting.

She accused him of trying to control her. Laying it all on her. Blaming her for things going wrong between them when it was his stark viewpoint that was ruining everything.

One night after sex, he wrote, he found himself reaching back into his memory. He began talking to her about his childhood again. She got up and went to the bathroom. She came back and stood looking out the window at the inner courtyard, the light from other apartments across her body, somebody watching football, a woman moving around a kitchen, the sound of a bottle being thrown into the bottle bank. Then she turned around and said, Fuck, Lukas, let it go.

She suggested therapy, but he refused to admit that he was the problem. He found himself taking fright at everyday things. City noise bothered him more than ever. A honking car-horn made him jump. A cyclist passing by without notice was like an attack. Even the squeak of a takeaway carton seemed to go off in his head like a siren.

He had stopped dreaming. He could not recall a single dream or nightmare in the past ten years. Like he was afraid of his own memory. Flinching from the past. His childhood had come between him and his life. All he could do on that night after the horse ran into the sea was to continue the ongoing process of self-storytelling. The unfinished construction of his biography, reassembling his memory like the furniture in a room.

It began with the dentist. The day of the man with the furry pink jacket, he was on his way to the dentist and tried to remember if it was the building with the dental surgery that was painted green or the building opposite. He could never remember which one it was. When he sat in the dentist's chair, half lying back with the plastic bib on, like a child, listening to the hygienist telling him where she went on holidays with her sister, he found himself looking at the building across the road. An old house with balconies built in. He was pretty sure it was painted green. Peppermint green. Pistachio peppermint ice-cream green. But this happened every time he went to the dentist. He came out and walked away and forgot to check if it was the building across the street that was painted green or the building with the dental practice on the first floor. He told himself each time to find out for certain. The problem was that by the time he got out of there, he was always glad to be free and failed to look.

The reason it mattered so much to him was that his mother once brought him to stay in a house that was painted green when he was around four years of age and she had to go into hospital for a series of tests. He could not remember being collected and brought home again. That meant, in some memory construction he had no control over, that he had been left there for ever. He could only remember being brought to the peppermint house, holding her hand as they walked along the path with roses on either side. His mother kissing him goodbye. He was crying because he felt the anxiety of his mother leaving her boy behind to go into hospital.

It felt as though he had been left in the peppermint-green house for the rest of his life. Letting go of the memory would have meant letting go of his mother's hand.

In the peppermint-green house, they said his mother was from somewhere else. She was an elsewhere woman and that meant he was an elsewhere boy, unable to speak like a normal child and say he needed to go to the bathroom. They put him into a cot with a rubber sheet. A rubber sheet that was dark red and squeaky and smelly and cold to touch.

They said he stank like an elsewhere boy. They opened the windows and the noise of traffic came in. You shitty little elsewhere boy, they said. He was brought into the big bathroom with the neon lights and the frosted windows and black and white tiles, like a chessboard. They undressed him and hosed him down with cold water. His lips went blue and they told him, Stop shivering like an elsewhere boy. They put him back in the cot with the rubber sheet with no trousers on while the other children were playing with toys in the same big room and the rosette on the ceiling had a long wire hanging down and a yellow bulb that had flies dancing up and down, chasing each other. The light was left on at night to make sure he stayed in the cot and didn't climb over the rails and run back to somewhere else. And even though he was not allowed to have any toys, a girl came over and gave him a train through the bars.

There was something else that he had previously written in his journal, perhaps once or twice before, maybe even several times more and had to write again, because it was such a formative experience. He was nine when his mother died and he was living with his father and his older brother Peter. He could remember a map of red dots on his father's wall. He had no idea what they were for, but they seemed terrifying. And one evening, his father brought him and his

43

brother to see an opera called *Don Giovanni*. The central character rejects the offer to repent and ends up walking into the flames of Hell. There was something glorious about disappearing into the fire. As a boy, he never quite understood the pain that went with being burned alive. Maybe it was more the sensation of guilt that his father passed on to him, like putting your finger into the flame of a candle multiplied by millions.

He held all those things in his head as a boy. The fire and the map of red dots on the wall of his father's office. Losing his mother seemed to have some connection with the red dots and maybe they eventually got into my lungs, he wrote. My lungs became my memory. The cause of my coughing and being unable to go to school. He began to put red dots into his schoolbooks. His history book, his math book, his copy books, all marked with a fine pattern, spreading like a virus drawn with a red pen. He went on to draw the dots on a bathroom wall at school, prompting an investigation in which all classes were suspended until the culprit owned up. He was silent under interrogation. The red dot scandal remained a mystery. It was not until his father came into his bedroom one evening and found that pattern of measles across the wall behind the door that the whole obsession came to light. He could remember his father shouting without any explanation – how dare you? How dare you show such disrespect?

And now, it seems, the red dots have got into the horse. The horse is full of my family grief. My history. A version of myself running into the sea to get away from the red dots on my father's wall.

He took the headphones off and decided to go out. He got dressed and put his shoes on. He left the key in the door of the room and walked along the hallway with the sand crunching underfoot. He heard the surfers as he passed by one of the rooms, like they were still surfing in their sleep.

He got to the reception desk and found the portrait of the German writer with the black beret looking at him with the cigarette dangling from his lips. The writer's eyebrows were sloping down at a sorrowful angle and maybe he belonged to a generation of people who had too much empathy. Coming from a time in which there was a terrible deficit in compassion, making up for it with a kind of empathy that was already gone out of fashion again in the twenty-first century. The writer's heart was shaped by tragic stories from the twentieth century that were no longer relevant. A sad, ironic look in his eyes that was based on a code of soft-hearted fellow feeling that seemed so outdated. As though traits like altruism were now replaced by self-care. Like all that compassion had turned into a general feeling of habitat loss and concern for the planet.

The moon was out.

He had been told by a friend who lived in Westport that it was good to drink water that contained moonlight. It was known, so his friend claimed, to stop the anxieties of the world getting to your heart. Night water, his friend told him, had healing qualities that were found in no other substance. You could take all the supplements, all the herbal remedies in the world, none of them came anywhere close to drinking water that contained the reflection of the moon. His friend, whom he had known in Berlin before he moved back to Westport, was in hospital right now on a course of preventive chemotherapy. He was planning to visit him as soon as he was discharged.

He grabbed a cup from the breakfast table and walked out into the night, hoping he didn't wake up the woman of the house, concealing the cup in the pocket of his jacket. He had the sudden feeling, as he walked through the hallway on his way out, that the writer had some duty to act as a reluctant security guard, checking everybody as they went out the door, letting the woman of the house know what frame of mind they were in and if they were a danger to themselves.

He closed the door behind him and made his way across the car park. Stopping suddenly with fright and turning around to see something moving behind him, he took a few cautious steps back to find out what it was. Then he leaped out of his skin when he saw five black shapes hanging on the line to dry. Five wetsuits with no faces and no hands and no feet. Like the surfers who had worn them had disappeared from the earth. The sea had taken them and dropped the suits back empty, leaving only a row of ghostly shells with flapping arms and dancing legs.

He continued walking as though he had become one of those hollow black suits. His face and hands gone white with the moon. As he came to the bog, the mournful sound of the accordion was louder than ever. Perhaps it was the motorbike with the older couple that he had seen earlier continuously travelling across the island unseen. The landscape was black and white, like one of those photographic negatives found among collections of old photographs in junk shops, everything in reverse, where the people had black faces and wore white clothes. He heard the scream of a nightjar. A black mound of turf appeared in the shape of a faceless creature asleep. Grasses like extra-large eyebrows in the breeze.

He came to a string of bog pools. The moon reflected on the surface turned the water to mercury. He took the cup from his pocket and scooped up some of water like an alchemist, holding it up to the moon to keep the silver level on top. With the silence of the bog around him, and the memory of Katia by the window, he began drinking the moon.

Seven

He sat at the breakfast table once more spreading a thin layer of marmalade over a slice of brown bread. The four golden pats of butter on a saucer were untouched as always. He had told the woman of the house that he didn't eat any dairy products and she looked at him as though he was undernourished. She continued to put the butter on the table each morning in case he changed his mind. The surfers were not up yet and he sat alone with the big Sacred Heart behind him on the end wall. He sent a message to his friend in Westport to say that he would be very happy to pick him up from the hospital and bring him home. His friend in Westport got back to say, thanks, he would let him know when he was being discharged.

The woman of the house came in with tea and said she heard him go out during the night. He told her that he went night walking. It's a thing people do, he said.

Like night swimming, she said.

No, night walking.

Walking was fine, she said, nothing wrong with that. Only night swimming was a concern, people had no idea of their own weakness with no clothes on.

He said he understood.

The sea is no fool, she added, looking into his eyes.

He smiled.

The sea had left seaweed draped over the boundary wall between the house and the strand. There was a buffer of sand left on the windowsills. Flecks of black seaweed had been pasted onto the windows and the waves were pounding the shore, like a fridge door being repeatedly closed.

Wild swimming, she said. That's what they call it.

He said in his own defence that he wasn't anywhere near the beach. He didn't do night swimming, only night walking. He said he walked up to the bog and the moon was out, it was almost like daylight.

Wild walking, she said.

No – just night walking. They all do it now in Berlin. To clear the head.

Is there something you're worried about?

Ah, the usual, he said. You know yourself.

No, I don't know.

His non-disclosure became a challenge. She sat down at the table opposite him, a guest in her own guesthouse. She sat sideways, he would later write in his journal, indicating that she only had a quick moment to hear what was on his mind that made him walk up to the bog of all places like a ghost.

Lukas, she said.

Yes.

The bog is not a safe place at night.

She may have looked out and seen him leaving at that late hour. She may have checked to see if he turned down towards the beach, just to make sure he was not a danger to himself. Wild walking out of the house at night with a cup in one pocket and his journal in the other, as though he couldn't be found dead without it. Curly hair. Straight back. Long thin legs striding into the calmness of the island night with the urgency of a city. Stopping to take fright at the soulless wetsuits hanging on the line. Then resuming his march off to the bog in the moonlight, as though he was part of a horror movie.

He asked her about the horse.

She knew that he was trying to divert her with horse questions.

McNally's horse had been bought from the Travellers, she said. They were here last summer. They stay on the sandy plain just beyond the petrol pumps. Some people say they came originally from the deserted village and they've been moving ever since, never settled again. I don't know if that's true or not, she said, but they like to come back every year to see the island and their children love the sea.

He wanted her to sit down properly, not sideways, have a cup of tea, why not, maybe join him for a slice of her own brown bread. She spoke to him with one hand on the table as though she was going to push herself off at any moment, just waiting for the right exit line.

Her husband appeared outside with a dustpan and brush, sweeping the sand off the windowsills. She knocked on the window and had a speechless conversation with him, pointing at the sky, it seemed, reminding him to remove the specks of seaweed that were stamped on the glass.

The boy loves that horse, she continued. McNally's grandson. His mother is a single mother, lived for a while in London, came back here just a few months ago.

He was waiting for her to lift off, but she stayed in position, not finished yet. She was giving him information that would have to be reciprocated. A trade in gossip that allowed no debts. She answered questions he didn't ask. The horse was going into the horsebox for the boy's safety. It was not in the boy's best interest to have such an unstable horse as a friend, with his mother just back from London. All the more so now that the horse went wild swimming without explanation.

I don't know what got into that horse, she said.

She looked at him with her head tilted to one side as though it was a question he needed to answer. Like there was something in his eyes that might disturb the tranquillity of the island.

When she finally lifted off with her hand pressing down on the table, she stood over him for a moment as though she already knew everything. He had the feeling that she could reach inside his mind and take out whatever she wanted. She knew perfectly well that his wife was not coming to join him. He was a young man, around fifty, in the depths of sorrow. One of those broken-hearted people. What else would have brought him to this island to be alone with beaches and cliffs and gannet colonies? Wild walking across the bog at night with a cup that he forgot to place back upside down like the rest. Drinking bog water and such nonsense, that was only going to make him sick.

She knew why he stood on the beach talking to the sea. She would be the first to tell him that the sea was not to be trusted. Don't listen to the sea, the woman of the house would be quick to tell him. You can't believe a word. She's had previous visitors at the guesthouse who took the sea at its word, people who believed everything they were told, and you don't want to know where they ended up.

He was the type of man who was still trying to come to grips with the history of his country. The inherited story of his people. An internal sort of man of few words. A non-surfer, if ever there was one. No thrill-seeker. Not searching for extreme experiences in the wild, apart from the extreme silence on the bog. Not a man who would dedicate his life to feats of endurance to prove his identity.

Not the type, for example, to go on a cruise. One of his friends in Berlin had invited him on a trip to the South Pole. Antarctica. The journey was all planned. December. They would travel from Berlin to Frankfurt and from there to Seattle. In Chile, they would join a ship that would take them down along the coast to Tierra del Fuego, a place of stunning emptiness. Then over to Port Stanley, a day's walking, and onwards to the ice. Colonies of penguins waiting to dive into the water. No polar bears, but plenty of sea birds, an albatross or two. And those enormous mountains of ice in front of you, hearing the explosion when a chunk the size of a building falls into the sea, like a disaster movie unfolding in front of your eyes.

He was more of a collector. The type of man who kept all kinds of useless memorabilia in his pockets. She had found him sitting at the breakfast table pulling out an old shopping list from the inside pocket of his jacket, the kind of thing that had by now become obsolete since people texted their shopping needs to each other on their phones.

A list in his hand that looked like some item recovered from a time before Gutenberg. Katia's beautiful hand-writing. A habit she must have inherited from her mother, from a country that no longer existed. An East German thing, perhaps, whereby she wrote out the things that were needed with enduring care, from a time when the words were as precious as the items themselves. The items had been purchased long ago – broccoli, pasta, pesto, muesli, toothpaste, filters size 2, don't forget. She spelt the word muesli incorrectly, a mild form of dyslexia.

It brought back the memory of the supermarket and the music that was playing while she phoned to add some female item she needed urgently and had forgotten to write down. Her inner face in the form of a scrapped shopping list. Her way of thinking, her point of view, her needs, her ambitions, the wide sweep of her desires and concerns, her love and her wish to be loved, moments of weakness and moments of triumph, that reckless sexual energy when she knew what she wanted most in the world. Her laugh. That little screech at the back of her throat.

He stored the shopping list in a pouch at the back of his journal, like a plundered possession. It turned him into a thief. Stealing from her. Stealing from himself.

Eight

All that silence, he said to the sea that morning while he was standing at the edge of the waves and the woman of the house was looking out the breakfast-room window.

The silence in my country and the silence between us. Katia and me not saying anything to each other. Like the sound had been turned off all over Berlin and the entire city had gone deaf. Nobody talking and nobody hearing anything.

The woman of the house was keeping an eye on him as though it was her duty to protect him, like a ward of court. Telling the sea to lay off, not to get any ideas.

He's not a surfer.

There is a unique word in German for silence, he told the bright green waves.

Schweigen.

The German word for silence is actually not that passive, he explained. It takes on a more proactive role. A loud kind of silence, full of intention. Not so much a base line emptiness but a situation in which information is being withheld.

In my language, he said to the sea, silence is not a substance or an absence but a cognitive activity, a verb rather than a noun, in which something is being consciously suppressed. Each country has its own silence. Each country has its own way of not saying things. And the German word *Schweigen*, or *Stillschweigen*, describes a kind of restraint. The act of silencing. Curtailing information. Creating a void.

We even have the imperative, he added, by which you can command somebody to be silent.

Schweig.

Hold your tongue. Be quiet. Become voiceless.

Every time he went into a café to read a newspaper in Berlin, he told the sea, there was something being kept silent. He would open up one of the free-to-read newspapers and find silence on every page. It was the same when he moved on to other news outlets, filled with news that was avoiding something. TV talk shows remembering things in order to un-remember other things. Empty spaces in debates where nobody spoke up for those with no voice. Podcasts that made people non-existent. The silence that originated between himself and Katia had spread across the entire country and left such a voiceless void in his head that he felt compelled to escape to the West of Ireland, to a place where he could tell the sea everything.

The listening sea.

While the woman of the house was still watching and the surfers were at the other end of the beach, he stood alone with the green waves turning white as they came up to his shoes and he was forced to jump back. Now and again, the sea began to dispute its own colour and claimed that the breakers curling in were more bottle green.

Perhaps it was the journal that caused the silence. Some intimate relationship he had with his journal that could not be matched by anyone in real life. His descriptions of Katia were more human than they could ever be while she was actually standing in front of him. Life had become more real in writing than it was in life. Nothing was true until it was recorded. The written circumstances more vivid, people more obedient, easier to manipulate in his journal than they might allow themselves to be in reality. Even sex became an act of storytelling, the precious details kept in a log. Her breasts described as the shape of cupped hands. His hair in the grip of her fist and his head thrown back as though he was decapitated.

The journal gave him an omniscient overview that separated him from the world and turned him into a witness rather than a participant. He was surprised sometimes that he had not told her something – did I not tell you that? It had already been written down in confidence. She was not the first receiver. His journal had become his true partner.

He could recall the moment, he said to the sea, when things came to a head between them. When she announced that she was leaving and made her departing speech. She was standing by the window once more, he said, looking at the trees in the inner courtyard. She was wearing her coat, like she had one foot out the door.

I'm never going to fit the person you want me to be, she said. I'm not the woman I was back then in the camper van. It was a great time, but that's not who I am. You don't know me, she said. You see me as this mythological figure from the past, Lukas. Some female goddess, elevated to a mythical level that is impossible to attain in a physical dimension. You love the ME in your fucking journal more than the ME in the room.

Lukas, you're a lovely man, she said, but it's like living under surveillance. You might as well be a CCTV camera that's never switched off, even at night in the bedroom. I can't even have a cry to myself without feeling overheard.

You know what? she said, turning around to look him straight in the eyes with a new defiance. I'm going to be ordinary. An ordinary woman, that's all I want to be.

She moved into an apartment not far away. Close to the hill where you can look down from Heaven over the city. She came back to get her things. She took the poster, the framed poster with the wanted sign, offering a reward for the return of a small painting of Francis Bacon that had been stolen from a gallery in Berlin. She left the round boulder they brought back from their honeymoon and took the unfinished face she had carved into a piece of oak, missing an ear. She took the brass Russian icon that a soldier had once worn around his neck and left what she called his precious manual coffee grinder that was about a hundred years old. And she took the photos. She deleted all those intimate photographs he had of her. My body is my copyright, she said. Liberating herself in a sweeping act of self-erasure.

She could not delete the undeletable descriptions in my journal. The memory of a bird we once found in the street. A fledgling kestrel, from the nest in the steeple of the church, a dark green wooden box that had been erected for them, above the clock with the golden hands. They must have got used to the bells ringing. From the café across the street, we often saw them on a ledge outside the green box and taking off to sweep across the churchyard. We heard them even when they were not seen, a threat call, somewhere between screeching and squeaking in the canopy. And sometimes a sighting of copper red wings hovering, the same colour as the copper red brickwork when the church was lit up in the sunshine. The fledgling kestrel was at street level, flapping its large wings, but it seemed to lack the trick of lifting off.

It crashed into the sides of the parked cars. I could think of no other way of rescuing it than to take off my jacket and fling it over the bird. We brought the kestrel back to our apartment and let it fly from the balcony.

We held it in our hands, he said to the sea, in a voice that was full of boyish wonder, warm and breathing hard, looking around with wild eyes, pecking at her arm. The heart beating so fast. We released it. Back into the wild, I suppose you would call it. Watched it fly across the courtyard and land in a walnut tree. It sat there for a while looking at us. Then it flew off, all along the interconnecting courtyards, up and away over the rooftops.

Months later, I ran into her in the street, and it looked as though I was stalking her. Had to tell her I was on my way to the dentist. I felt like a passing pedestrian in her presence, he said. She was so polite. She smiled and said she was in a hurry back to work.

She was wearing black trousers with gold thread woven through the fabric and a white shirt that showed her bra strap underneath. She had blue paint on her hands. Her hair matched her new independence, cut straight across the top of her forehead in what she calls the Berliner Pony.

She seemed more real than ever, he said to the bottle-green sea, more Katia than he could remember. I found myself trying to hold on to her physical presence like you could capture it in a perfect sentence.

I have to run, she said.

She turned her back and walked away, he said to the sea. I was hoping she would turn around, maybe blow a kiss with her thumb. The thumb kiss she used to throw to places where we slept together. Bars we had once been in got the thumb kiss when we passed by. The place where David Bowie used to hang out got a treble thumb kiss.

No thumb kiss, he told the waves.

Our silence was not like the silence on the bog at night. Not the uplifting silence of nature, filled with tiny components of sound, like the distant call of a fox or a dog barking in the valley or the squeak of a gate banging in the wind. Not that silence full of volume that you get in the wild, when you're listening out for things right behind you in the dark.

The silence in our country was a dead silence. An airborne silence that got into every corner of the city. Something left unspoken, in the streets, in the shops and supermarkets, in bars and cafés, in apartment blocks. A vast emptiness at the heart of the city that you found in the eyes of the people passing by, in the park where they played football, under bridges where lovers clamped padlocks to the railings. Where a mother stood with a boy on the way home from school to watch a train slipping by underneath like a snake. Where he got that dizzy sensation in his feet and the thrill of falling in his stomach. Where the sun was tilted at a reckless angle and the metal beams of the bridge cast enormous shadows across the pavement. Where the feeling of vertigo had nothing to do with height or depth or gravity or the illusion created by crows wheeling around below but the overwhelming sense of things screaming to be said.

Nine

If memory had a physical shape, it would look like a deserted village.

He got there in the afternoon. It was a fine day and there was a slight breeze coming in from the sea that filled his shirt like a balloon. The deserted village was unchanged from the time he had been there with Katia, only perhaps that it was now all the more deserted.

The sun was sloping across the stone walls of homes long abandoned. Some overgrown with grass and moss. Rows of fallen walls receding into the past. No roofs. No furnishings. No artefacts. Only the gable ends managing to stand up to the wind. Here and there a shelf built into the interior wall where they must have kept the eggs or the butter. A lintel still intact and a small tree growing where an entire family used to huddle together in one bed to keep warm and stop coughing.

It was not the village that had been deserted, he told

himself to write in his journal. It was the other way around. The village had lost the ability to sustain its inhabitants. They were the forsaken people. Their view of the sea and the mountains had been extinguished along with their names. All that was left was the memory of them in the shape of a scattered village, disappearing into the deep retention of the mountain.

At the gable end of one of the homes, there was a flat rock, like a stone sofa. Where the old people must have sat on a fine day looking across the bay at the cliffs and the men out fishing. A good place to watch families gathering seaweed to spread onto the potato drills as fertiliser and collect the news coming from the shore. The silence was absolute in that forgotten place. Nothing but a soft wind brushing the grasses and blowing through gaps in the stone walls. A stream running along the path whispering in a lost language.

A skeleton of human habitation, so the German writer with the black beret had written in his journal back in the last century when he came to the island to be healed after the war. The revolutionary writer with his outmoded empathy shaped by the tragedy of war and people emerging from the rubble. The writer whose books were once read all over the world and whose sense of compassion and moral concern were no longer in demand. The man with the black beret who got into a fight with his own country and became a stranger in his own life. These ruins, the writer wrote in his travel essays, recalled the post-war design of devastated cities in his own country where there was nothing left but the most deadly silence.

He recalled reading a book in which the writer with the black beret described a character among the ruins after the war. A home that looked like the cross-section of a doll's house, with the furniture still intact, a bath filled up, a sewing machine with a boy's trousers in mid stitch. Going through the shell of the house to see what could be salvaged, the character, who might well have been the author, found himself in front of a mirror. He could not face the sight of his own face. In a moment of extreme self-loathing, he picked up a hammer and smashed the mirror. His own reflection shattering into a thousand shards among the ruins.

A hundred years later, these ruins in the West of Ireland looked more like ruins of recent wars. Cities that looked like X-rays and could have been mistaken for photographs of previous wars and inspired a kind of compassion that was out of synch with the time. Schools and playgrounds and empty apartment blocks. A mouth with lots of missing teeth.

These stone ruins of a deserted village no longer appeared like they belonged to the past. He was not looking at the shape of memory. He was looking at what was happening in the present. These ruins now spoke of all the migration and people fleeing across the world today.

He thought of buses with children waving out the window. Lovers matching hands through glass panes. People carrying all they owned in suitcases and Ikea bags tied with string. Images that were old and new at the same time, like the photos his father used to show him of people, including his own ancestors, who had had to flee their homes in previous wars. People taking the most essential things with them – a hairbrush, a nail file, a pencil case, scissors, a butter dish. Possessions wrapped in a bed sheet and carried on a stick. Bicycles with a suitcase on each of the handlebars. Some came with no more than the shoes they walked in. And the mud underfoot. An overcoat that functioned as a home, a bed, a blanket, a roof over your head, all in one. Some brought only the most personal items – a diary, a bundle of love letters, the story of what was left behind.

And maybe, he wrote later, the ruins looked like a vision of the future when all trace of human life is gone.

He recalled an image of war that he had recently seen online. A photo from a war zone that had nothing to do with the red dots in history but just happened to come from the same country as the red dots.

The image was that of a dead soldier. Killed in combat. Lying on his back on a gravel road, flattened into the earth by passing trucks. The soldier had virtually disappeared under the heavy pounding of military traffic. His head and hands no longer visible. A trespassing conscript lying out on a country road with no houses in sight. No more than a tattered uniform laid out in a location between destinations, far from home and nowhere near anywhere. The boots still attached in good condition, above ground, hanging on by the soles of his feet as though the dead soldier still had a delicate foothold in the living world.

Dead uniform with boots attached, is how he described it in his journal.

A two-dimensional memorial. A surface man, ironed out by tanks and vehicles with big wheels carrying soldiers who gave out a cheer each time they ran over him. The ignominy of his death was like some Greek tragedy in which he had been condemned to die over and over again each day for all eternity. The flat-pressed regalia with army-issue boots still on and a wasted notion of national pride in his buried head. The photograph was all that remained, passed around on social media, waiting to be utterly forgotten. Perhaps he was wearing one of those brass icons that were meant to spare his life and somebody ripped from his neck before he was buried under the traffic.

The ocean had turned into a sheet of grey cloth.

Mossy floor, he later wrote. A million years under my feet. Couple of clouds. Wind across my chest. Human voice of a lamb on the mountain calling. View across the bay and the distant coastline.

On the way back he saw the couple on the motorbike passing by once more. He had seen them earlier on and they now passed him by in the exact same spot. The woman on the back waved at him as before. And this time he waved back, because they were familiar to him, even though he never got talking to them. It felt as though he was retracing his steps, each time he went out walking. No matter where he went, the couple turned up either ahead of him or from behind. He would hear the sound of the accordion some distance away and he could already tell they were coming. They wore no helmets. The man driving the motorbike wore a cap turned backwards. The woman wore retro sunglasses with pointed wings, making the landscape more like some part of California, perhaps. She had white hair and a red scarf flowing behind her like a flag. They seemed not to have any particular destination to get to, only joyriding around the island in a loop.

When he got back to the guesthouse, he asked the woman of the house about them. They were a German pair who had moved to the island from Bavaria, living at the far end near the bridge. About ten years ago, the woman of the house said, the woman on the back of the motorbike returned home to get an operation done on her legs. She had trouble with her veins, so the surgeons over there operated on her, but the surgery, some kind of liquid treatment whereby the affected veins dissolve and disappear, was unsuccessful.

They managed to destroy a lot of the nerves in her legs. Nothing could be done, she said, because you have to sign a pre-op document saying you understand the risks involved. The poor woman, so the woman of the house said, has been living in constant pain ever since. They're in their late sixties now. Not a day goes by that she isn't in agony. They've tried everything. All kinds of pain counselling. She distracts herself with painting. But the pain is there all the time. You'd never know by looking at her, the woman of the house said, because she's always smiling and letting on it doesn't hurt. The happiest person on earth, you would think when you meet her. Only the pain is horrendous. That's the only word for it, so her husband says. Absolutely horrendous. Like she has been cursed to endure this lifelong agony.

The only thing that works, the woman of the house said, is when she's on the motorbike. It's a combination of the way she sits on the back of the bike, the positioning of her legs and the throbbing of the engine that instantly makes the pain go away. That's why they keep driving around all the time without stopping. He loves her and he'll drive her anywhere she wants to go. They never stop to get off and look at the view, only driving up and down the island to keep the pain away.

Ten

The horse stood with its back to the sea. There was a bandage around its neck, strapped with two leather belts. It stood close to the barn, dipping its head down from time to time into a bucket on the ground, with the never-ending sound of the sea coming across the stone walls. With bandaging around the neck that appeared to be covered with a tea towel, the horse looked as though it had escaped from the *Guernica* painting and left the trauma of war behind. Back to this sanctuary by the sea where it was given a feed of oats.

The sea was loud. Raucous and rowdy. A mess of choppy waves and no boats out. Cursing and swearing and spitting bits of seaweed on the wind.

Dirty day, according to the woman of the house.

The sea growled and didn't think much of drinking moon water. Stop deluding yourself with shamanic notions,

Lukas. Listen to the woman of the house, she knows. She's seen them coming here trying to escape from themselves. They end up sitting on the edge of the cliffs with the gannet colony like it's the end of the world. They find some enormous emptiness inside themselves and step into the enormous emptiness of the water. The last man to give himself to the deep was staying at the guesthouse in the same room, number nine.

The surfers were nowhere to be seen. Their wetsuits were taken in off the line but there would be no need to put them on because the waves were not clean. The woman of the house was now hanging out sheets and towels, watching him from a distance as he spoke to the sea, and the sea was responding with debris delivered from the deep.

He jumped when he got the buzz in his pocket and took out his phone. A call from Katia. At last, he said to the sea. Her image turning up on his phone was a lifeline. Her voice made him nauseous with hope.

Out there with all that noise, he couldn't hear a word at first. She said she couldn't hear him either, was he having a shower or something? He was tempted to call her back but he didn't want to hang up. He stepped away from the edge of the water and took a few paces back towards the guesthouse.

Her voice brought such an instant physical longing that he could not hold back a surge of sexual images.

Her breath made him recoup the most graphic memories. Mostly from behind, with her back turned. The back of her knees. Dimples on her lower back. Her arse wrapped in white cotton as she walked across the room. Tattoo of a lizard crawling along her shoulder, left of the spine, as she lay face down on the bed. And, of course, the most enduring image of all, the one that he remembered best and described many times in his journal, of her pulling up her trousers. That dance of departure. The striptease in reverse, he called it. Revoking her body in slow, incremental, mind-blowing flashes.

She was calling about Emilia.

Emi.

She doesn't eat properly, Katia said. She's got thin. Her face is pale. I cook her favourite dinner, you know, ramen with chicken. She doesn't touch it. She puts her spoon in and turns things over like she's examining the contents of a witch's cauldron. Then she meets her friends to eat *pommes frites*.

Pommes.

I want you to speak to her, she said.

At least she's eating something.

Pommes, she said, in a screech that could well be heard by the sea and the woman of the house. That's not food.

You love *pommes*, he said.

She ignored that remark.

Pommes frites with a sprinkle of paprika across the top and lots of salt. Mayonnaise and ketchup.

She accused him of paying no attention to what she was calling about. He had no idea what it was like to bring up a teenage daughter who didn't eat properly. Girls don't eat now. They starve themselves for some reason, then eat in secret. And who knows what company she might be sharing her *pommes* with?

Are you still tracking her?

No. She doesn't allow that.

She needs her privacy, he said.

All she ever does is complain, Lukas. She's picked that up from you. All day long, she throws these doom facts around, like it's my fault. What can I do? I have my own trouble with this tribunal of inquiry and she's starting to get involved in all that protesting. I'm doing my best to keep her positive, but it's not easy. I need your help.

For a moment, at least, he still mattered to her as a parent. He felt he was back in her innermost thoughts. Their minds still functioned as one. He told her that he had invited Emilia over to Ireland to take up surfing, but what he would like best was to be back in Berlin sharing a little basket of *pommes*, with mayonnaise and two little wooden forks.

You can't live on *pommes*, she said. Here, Lukas, you talk to her.

Emilia came on after a pause in which he heard them having a verbal scuffle.

Hi, Dad.

What's this about *pommes*?

His daughter told him that her mother had gone a bit weird, that was the only word for it. Her level of disgust had gone through the roof, she can't even stand a cup in the sink any more. She gives out to me for leaving a little kink in the shampoo bottle after a shower, she said. It's meant to be found by the next person as though it hasn't been used by the last person. Imagine, she said. And as for underwear on the floor, that's become a crime against humanity.

He loved his daughter's ironic voice.

Her mother, she said, was working on a painting that basically looked like a large vagina. I don't know what's come over her, Emi said. I think she's losing it since this whole *Guernica* thing happened and she's waiting for the decision to fall one way or the other on whether she still has a job. She needs a new therapist. Disgust counselling, that's what she needs.

Don't be mean, he said.

His daughter said it was no joke. Her mother's painting looked like a vagina but was, in fact, an open throat. She took a photo of my larynx, his daughter said, and now it's become this piece of art. Nobody is going to be able to tell the difference between my larynx and my vagina.

Emi, please, he said.

It's all about free speech, Emilia said.

Your throat?

She's using my larynx as a symbol of free speech.

That's a good idea, he said.

Yeah, but listen, Dad. She's now posted that photo on Instagram. You must have seen it. My larynx is all over the place. I swear. Everybody thinks it's my vulva.

He tried to get back to the subject of proper nutrition. Why was she rejecting her mother's food? Did it have to do with their separation? Was it all a bit too close, the two of them in one apartment? Some need to get away from her mother's surveillance? He could not help seeing a chain of *pommes frites* slowly, nonchalantly, with maximum glower, making their way into his daughter's mouth. Thousands of little sticks tipped with mayonnaise, some with ketchup, some with both. Eating and talking. Entrance. Exit. That dual-purpose tool for language and food. No stopping the *pommes* going into her mouth and no stopping her saying what she wanted to say.

Don't go out hungry, he said.

Emilia ignored that useless advice and handed the phone to her mother. Katia's voice came back and it seemed, while they were talking, at least, that everything could still be the same between them. Being separated was just another form of being together. They were still co-parenting. Her voice seemed to signal that she might be open to getting together again, or maybe not completely shutting herself off.

How are you? he asked her.

I'm fine, she said.

Is everything OK?

Everything is fine, she said. Apart from Emi. Honestly. She's driving me crazy.

It's the tribunal, he said. The uncertainty of it.

She's not helping one bit, Katia said.

There was a long pause in which she might have been watching Emilia going into the kitchen for another snack or she might have been waiting for him to say more.

I love you, he said.

He was trying hard not to sound like a pop song.

You're my most …

He could not find the right superlative.

That's not your chocolate, she said.

She was talking to Emilia.

Put that back.

He waited for her to respond to his words.

Jesus, that girl, she said.

At least they were breathing together on the phone. Still holding hands on roaming. He wanted to say that he couldn't get her out of his mind. He wanted to ask her if she was seeing somebody, but he didn't want to know. He wanted to say that even talking to her about their daughter's eating habits meant everything to him.

I miss you, Katia, he said.

He was hoping she would say something in return, but then he heard her arguing with Emilia again. It seemed as though she had put the phone down on the kitchen countertop and got into a physical scuffle over the chocolate. Or maybe she was holding the phone away from herself at arm's length as she got into another heated debate with her daughter, both of them shouting across the room at each other and a door closing with a bang, while he became a silent spectator, dropping out of contact with the Atlantic growling in the background and the woman of the house appearing between two hanging towels.

He walked along the shore. He needed to be in motion. He could not help seeing Katia standing at a fast-food stall, her elbow leaning on a high table. The small wooden fork in her fingers. The bright light of the overhead display on her face. People looking up at the menu. The various deals and combinations on offer. The sound of voices and humming and traffic and bottle tops and fizz and stainless-steel baskets rattling in stainless-steel containers and mayonnaise or ketchup and that will be six fifty and thank you and a smile handed down from above. Somebody standing close with a paper cup and Katia putting the other hand in her pocket and the night still ahead on the street with the bar called after a female singer from the last century. People in groups and people alone and bins filling up and somebody coming through on a bike and Katia moving aside with her hair tied up and long earrings and the collar of her jacket raised after the theatre, spearing two or three of the *pommes frites* with her fork and dipping them into the mayonnaise and bringing them up to her mouth, the entrance to her heart.

Eleven

He ran into one of the surfers. It was the woman with the aquamarine eyes. She was in bare feet, wearing an open jacket. She came up to face him and said there was a baby seal on the beach. She pointed to the far end and said it might be better for him not to go down that direction. If you get too close, she said, the mother will not come back and collect her baby. He thanked her for letting him know and saw what looked like a grey boulder thrown up by the sea in the shape of a seal.

She introduced herself as Taylor from Vancouver with Irish ancestors. He gave his name and shook her hand. An open smile both ways and her blue eyes were the colour of the sea. As though her face was printed on a sheet of cardboard with two holes where the sea could peer through.

The worst thing is people with dogs, she said. The dog runs up and sniffs at the seal and the mother then won't come back, definitely.

There was no dog on the beach.

She asked him if he was a surfer and he shook his head. He said it was not something he had ever had time to get into. He was more of a walker, bogs, mountain roads, cliffs, that was plenty for him, he said.

You don't know what it's like, she said, until you've experienced it for yourself.

I know, he said. Looks great.

It's that rush you get on top of the wave.

She laughed at him, like a boy who had never tried alcohol or smoked a joint. Like she was there to tempt him and he was too afraid to try it.

Believe me, she said. You have not lived until you take to the waves.

He felt that she was standing a little too close. The open-ended beach in both directions seemed to have become more of an indoor space. Her eyes were full of inquisition, pinning him back with a gaze that was both provocative and innocent at the same time. He found himself trying to back away without making it obvious. He was doing his best not to glance at her surfer's body. She crossed her arms and tilted her head, aware and unaware of the blue depth in her eyes, just calmly watching his male thoughts darting for cover like rabbits.

Out there on the wave, she said, is better than any drug you can get. It's profound. It's psychedelic. It's visionary. Totally mind-blowing.

He smiled and said he could well believe it.

That might have sounded to her like dismissal. Vague words to try and bring the conversation to an end.

Out there, she said, with renewed vehemence, you lose any sense of gender. You become a higher being. Out of this world, Lukas.

It was the way she used his name that made her seem so physically close. The advisory tone in her language. The persuasive power in her eyes. Like she knew he was on the loose, out there alone on an island with all that beauty around, ready for a new adventure.

She said she worked in a stressful job in the airline industry and this was the only thing that truly gave her peace. And because he didn't say much in response, she began to speak for him, putting words in his mouth.

You're going to love it, Lukas.

Soon as he made the decision to become a surfer, and she seemed to have made that decision for him right there with the sea behind her matching the colour of her eyes, he would be a changed man. She made him feel more athletic, more like a man who was up for a bit of fun. Perhaps she took him as younger than his fifty years, maybe even single. This might be a turning point in his life, like it was a turning point in her life. It would get rid of all his existential anxieties. All his concerns about himself and the planet and the shit that was going on in the world.

Maybe that's what I need, he said.

One of the guys will lend you a wetsuit.

All he had to do, she told him, was to get his own board. In Westport, on the street close to the clock tower, same side as the shop on the corner that sold lots of souvenirs and toys, everything from umbrellas to hats and fishing rods and ornamental walking sticks, even a little plastic fire engine for kids, there was a sports shop that sold all kinds of walking boots and thermal outdoor gear, and a couple of boards, she said.

While he was listening to her instructions, it seemed as though he had already agreed to become a surfer. Already thinking of what he might look like in photographs on the beach with a surfboard under his arm and the string attached to his ankle, lying on his belly waiting for the right wave, his own little heroic act of staying on top.

It's like being part of a family, she said. We're all part of the same earth. We all have this collective human consciousness. We share the same air. We share this planet and the waves and each other. We're free to be who we want and be with who we want. Out there, she went on to say, it's all love.

Sure, he said.

He turned his head inland, an expression of doubt. Like he was clinging to the safety of the earth. He could see the woman of the house standing with an empty laundry basket in her hand, looking at him talking to the surfer as though he was lost now and might become one of that free-love, polyamorous, pan-gender family of surfers, like you never knew who was who and what bed they were in and what rules of cohabitation they lived by as long as they didn't make too much noise or keep the non-surfing guests awake at night.

Come and join us, the woman with the aquamarine eyes said. You'll get the hang of it. We sometimes go elsewhere along the coast to chase the big ones, the real barrel waves. But here is good. You lie on your board waiting for the right wave. The sea is trying to hide itself until the very last minute, but in the end, you will always find your wave, Lukas.

I get it, he said.

Once you stand up on that wave, she said, you experience a kind of connection with the sea and the planet and the rest of humanity that feels transformative. Like your entire brain is being rewired. I'm telling you, Lukas. It's life-changing. Like, have you ever taken Molly?

Yes, he said.

In Berlin, in the clubs?

He nodded.

That's what it's like, she said. It blows your mind.

He wondered how she knew he was from Berlin. Perhaps the woman of the house had told her.

You're on this love drug and the crowd is surging around you. All those bodies jumping up and down. You love everybody and everything in sight. Out there on the wave, you enter into that kind of spiritual state of intense being. It's a mystical experience, Lukas. I don't mean mystical in any religious sense. It's more, like, deep. It opens up your mind, like a telescope turned inside. Like you find galaxies inside yourself that were previously unknown. You are connected to the universe and you get this overwhelming feeling of infinite love coming towards you.

She may have blown it at that point.

It seemed as though she was still trying to sell the concept of surfing to herself. Like she needed to convert him in order to justify her own beliefs. She could not bear to see the loneliness of a non-surfer. Not until she had brought him into the family of surfers, not until she had conquered him like a wave, could she let go and be a true surfer herself.

I'm heading in to Westport right now, he told her.

Great.

She winked at him and he smiled back.

I'm on my way to collect a friend of mine. He's in hospital.

Sorry to hear that, she said.

Yeah, thanks, but he's getting out. Brush with cancer. He's OK now. Looks like he's beaten it.

That's good to know.

The mention of illness brought the world back to normal. The euphoria of surfing and love with the sea appeared to fade a little in her eyes. A shade darker blue. As he later wrote in his journal, the word hospital might have broken a spell of some sort. The flow of attraction had been momentarily suspended by the awareness of suffering. It shattered the illusion of complete health and well-being that came from such a trance-like relationship with the waves.

She remained full of optimism and hope that she had converted him to the living, the non-dying, non-hospitalised people of this earth, and that he already belonged to a community beyond pain.

She embraced him like a surfer. He had seen them in the pub, frequently embracing each other, sometimes adding high-pitched expressions of joy that he envied and mistrusted simultaneously. He had even seen somebody standing on a surfer's bare foot and the surfer jumping back with a yelp, then attempting to embrace the man who had stood on his foot with a boot covered in cement, just to say that everything was fine, no harm done. He saw them sometimes in group hugs, three or four in one embrace with touching heads.

She moved forward and threw her arms out to signal that the embrace was coming. Giving him time to adjust and be ready to enter into the surfer's hug. A symbolic gesture of friendship as much as a physical affirmation of instant membership. That first touch meeting in the open to prove that the world was full of friendship and it was good to be alive right now. Her body leaning into his for a moment, a tap on the back, then pushing off again in the same continuous flow of acrobatic energy. He felt the cushioned contact in his chest before she pulled back and smiled. Then she turned and walked away with her bare feet slapping the foam of the spent waves. The seal was gone. The mother must have come back to collect her baby.

Twelve

He had not touched the hired car since he arrived and there was already a thin layer of sand covering the maroon and white paintwork. Designed like a runner without shoelaces, is how he described it in his journal. Footwear on wheels. The registration plate showing like a brand name on the heel.

Off you go now, the sea said. Go and be like one of the surfers. Come back with your surfboard full of happiness and spiritual explanations.

The sea went out of sight on the right-hand side. He came to the bog and stopped in a place where emigrants in the old days used to turn around and get the last view of home before it disappeared.

The place of last looking back is what the woman of the house called it.

She told him to look out for a spot along the road where the people leaving on the bus to Westport for the train looked back to catch that last sighting of home. One of the more unknown landmarks. A place where passengers turned around to see that final view of the mountains before the island vanished. Sometimes the bus would stop briefly and allow this moment of visual departure to take place before it moved on again and the passengers would in that moment have turned into strangers. That point in the landscape where people travelling abroad became separated from their homes and families and the landscape in which they had grown up. One or two of the passengers, hard men who brushed off the pain of leaving, would bitterly refuse to look around, so the woman of the house said. Men who didn't give in to their emotions. Only in the songs they sang when they were drunk in whatever place they ended up. That place of last looking back was like the point of death. The rear view became the confirmation of exile, the moment when the mountains and the people vanished from your life.

He did what the woman of the house said and stopped the car at the place of last looking back. She said he would recognise it because it was after a long stretch of straight road across the bog, before the bend in the road took him into a different terrain of fields and the inlet where the salmon farms had been set up. If you saw the salmon farms, you had already gone past and missed it, she told him.

People travelled back and forth across that place of last looking back every day now, she said, and they don't give it a second thought, let alone stop and think about what might have gone missing. And maybe, the woman of the house said to him, the whole idea of homesickness is not relevant any more, like it's a feeling that's gone out of date, now that people can phone and see each other on Zoom calls any time of the day. It might have stopped being such a painful place now and there were other ways of last looking back.

He stood on the road and took in that emigrant view, where the mountains were still in sight. Before the point where he disappeared from the earth and maybe it was the mountains that were left grieving for all those people who had vanished over the years. All the familiar faces of people who had walked there once and never come back.

He felt a sickness in his stomach. A feeling of vertigo in his heart that came out in one gush of brown bog water. The sickness of leaving. The sickness of no returning. The sickness of last looking back.

He got the smell of turf burning. A sweet scent that was not unlike the smell of the cigars he remembered his uncle smoking over a game of chess on Saturday afternoons with his father, all downcast eyes on the board and the visibility in the room so poor the opponents could hardly see each other with the smoke. The horse was right. There was a thin blue fog hanging in the air in a place with no houses and no chimneys. A subterranean fire spreading under the surface without a flame in sight.

Back in the car, he stared at the blue smog. Cars were passing by mostly in the direction of Westport and nobody stopping to look back. He saw the German couple on the motorbike once more, coming in the opposite direction as if they were crossing the meridian between home and away. They disappeared into the thin blue smoke that was now beginning to erase that final view of the island.

He drove on into the vanishing world. That moment of departure in which he was leaving his previous life behind and entering into the unknown. The portal of exile through which he would cross into a new version of himself, a surfer full of adventure and ubiquitous freedom. He would discover happiness. He would live in a community of extreme love. Be embraced by the sea. He would re-enter the world with no memory, no fear of looking back at what was left behind.

Perhaps the world was full of exiled people now. Everybody gone past the point of looking back. Those who left and those who stayed behind. Those who migrate with their feet and those who migrate with their heads. Like we all come from elsewhere now and nobody is completely at home.

He found himself imagining his own mother leaving home. She must have had a moment of last looking back in the land of red dots where she came from. He had a photograph of her around the time that his father must have met her first. A young woman, before she was married. Before she was a mother. She was dressed in a brown coat and a black scarf wrapped around her neck. The photo must have been taken in winter. She was smiling and her shoulders were up against the cold. She left home without saying goodbye to anyone. Letting them know that she was leaving would have put an end to her plans. The authorities would have come to arrest her and she would never have seen his father again. She had met him while she was working at the town hall. He had gone there to research the red dots and she helped him with some information, pulling out the archives for him. She went walking with him around the town and they made a plan for her to take the train to the coast, to one of the tourist resorts. He would meet her there and take her to Germany.

When he was a boy, she had once told him about that train journey, how frightened she was of being stopped by the authorities and the plan might fail. He remembered her telling the story as though there was a possibility all along that she might not have been his mother and he might never have existed. She had a holdall bag with her belongings. The station was empty and she was afraid somebody would come and ask where she was going. On the train, she remembered a family who had brought their dog and they had a small board game to keep themselves occupied. She was sitting by the window and somebody had mistaken her holdall bag for their own and she had to fight for it back.

The journey was like waiting in motion. Waiting for the moment when she could look back at the place she would never see again. It was the unknown place ahead that she was thinking of rather than what was gone out of sight for ever. And perhaps the moment of last looking back only happened later, when she was telling him, as a boy, about that journey. When she was already ill and told him the story of her escape and how he looked just like one of her uncles back in the country she came from.

He had inherited that feeling of last looking back. It was passed on to him as a child. The experience of coming from somewhere else, a place that was gone out of sight but never forgotten.

Thirteen

He drove with the windows open. He passed yellow signs depicting a graphic of a car veering off the road. A warning to motorists not to fall asleep or you might end up in the bog and be found a few centuries later perfectly preserved, your withered hands still gripping the steering wheel. Before you went on display in a gallery of bog bodies, they would examine the contents of your stomach to find out that you were a visitor from Berlin, a man with a troubled heart and no food in his belly apart from a little dribble of bog water.

He stopped at a supermarket along the way to get a bottle of still water. He opened it as he came out of the shop and it tasted like bog water but at least it was clear and not brown and full of moonlight.

A group of mothers with buggies stood outside talking to each other. One of them appeared to be saying something grotesque and the others opened their mouths in disgust.

One of them recoiled and turned away so disgusted by what the other mother was saying that she was about to get sick, only that she then turned around and wanted more. One of the mothers threw her head back, making a face of inspired revulsion. Another mother was so repulsed by the information that she began laughing, a shriek that was almost joyous. The mother who was describing the object of disgust felt encouraged by their reactions to continue. It was so truthful that she had no choice but to tell it in the most glorious details.

I swear to God, he briefly heard the mother who was relating the object of disgust saying as he passed them by. He could not very well linger and listen in to find out what it was they were so disgusted by and had to continue making his way back to the car. The mother resumed talking to the other mothers once he got back into his car and he envied their ability to be appalled in such a rapturous way. Like you had to be a young mother with a buggy to be entitled to hear this stuff. It was so disgusting only they could understand.

When he got into Westport, he parked the car close to the courthouse and walked around the streets. He came to the corner shop and walked inside. He loved the confused disarray of merchandise, everything from books and magazines to souvenirs and toys. On one of the walls, there was a selection of plastic flowers. In another corner, he found food containers. Another part of the shop was devoted to umbrellas and plastic ponchos. He moved on to the sports shop a couple of doors up with a good selection of outdoor gear and walking boots. He came across the surfboards at the back of the shop. One of them in light blue with a design of shark's teeth and a large, slightly amusing shark eye. There was a second board decorated with an Aboriginal design.

He stood looking at this minimal selection when he got a video call from his daughter.

Emilia.

At first, he saw nothing but people in motion. The view was shaky and tense. An underground station with people talking and shouting. Some of the voices were panicking and some of the voices were telling people to calm down. He recognised the name of the underground station and knew it was a junction between two lines, where people could hop off one train and get on another just across the platform, where he once kissed Katia a fraction too long and she just about got on her train in time before the doors closed on a bit of her coat and she pulled it in after her. He caught a glimpse of posters on the walls – a man on a running track, they were advertising high-end running shoes.

Emi, he called once more. He walked out of the shop, a non-buyer. He went out on the street and continued watching his phone.

He could see people in the underground station heading towards the exit, moving up the stairs, somebody at the top in an official voice telling them to keep to one side and leave the other free for rescue services. Everything is under control, the voice kept saying. No need to panic. Then the voice suddenly told everyone to stand still, not to move until they were told to. People were holding up their phones like they were at a concert. A woman said, This is the last time I'm getting the U-Bahn.

A younger woman could be seen turning around, flicking her hair back and telling the older woman to shut up and stay at home in future. We don't want you on the underground fouling up our stuffy air.

I felt powerless, he later wrote in his journal. Standing outside a shop with rain gear hanging in the doorway, looking at a live crisis on the underground in Berlin.

On the other side of the stairs, he could see paramedics running down in the opposite direction.

Dad, is that you? he then heard Emilia saying.

Are you OK?

Jesus, Dad. Yes, we're OK.

She turned the video around and allowed him to see her face.

There's been a human incident. Oh, my God, you should have seen it, blood everywhere.

Somebody in the crowd behind her was getting sick and

everybody, as a result, was not only moving away from whatever human incident had taken place but also from the sound of a woman vomiting.

He could not trust what he was seeing. As if this was all being made up, some pre-recorded scenes that were now being played back to him. It was a shock to realise that this was all happening live.

Is your mother with you?

No, Emilia said.

Did you tell her that you're OK?

Sure, of course I did. There's no panic, Dad. It's all over now. Jesus, you should have seen it. People screaming.

What happened?

This guy jumped in front of the train. It was awful. We heard the noise, Dad. The crack of his body. The crunch of his bones. Oh, my God. And the screech of the wheels.

Was he wearing a furry jacket?

I don't know. She turned away to ask. Was he wearing a furry jacket?

A pink furry jacket, he said.

I don't know. I just saw him jumping off the platform, that's all I saw.

Pink jacket.

What pink jacket?

The man who got killed, he said. I saw him once, Emi. Jumping down on the tracks. He was wearing a pink jacket.

A refugee, probably from some war zone. Like he must have gone through something awful to do that to himself. A pink jacket, like a pink bomber jacket?

Jesus, Dad, I can't believe you're asking me this. Who cares what he was wearing? He's fucking dead.

I've seen him, he said. Tall man with a furry jacket that's too small for him.

Do you want me to go back and check what kind of jacket he had on?

No, Emi. As long as you're safe, that's all that matters.

He realised how disconnected he might have sounded to her right then, standing on a street in the West of Ireland with tourists going by, asking his daughter if the man she saw getting hit by the train was the same man he had once seen not getting hit by the train.

I want to give you a big hug, he said.

It's scary, Dad.

Good to know you're safe, Emi.

In a flash memory, he thought of a time of safety, when she was a child and he was able to watch over her, when she woke up at night, and he would place his hand on her tummy, nothing more, no talking, just a hand on her tummy, then she went back to sleep again. And the time they were in a playground and he had to stand beside her like a security guard while she was eating a doughnut because there was a sign on the gate that said, Beware of crows stealing from the children.

The camera then turned to another young woman.

This is Amanda, his daughter said.

He found himself talking to Emilia's friend. She was smiling, utterly calm and in command, like an older sister.

Emi is OK.

We're just calling to let you know that everything is fine, nothing to worry about. There was a human incident on the platform, on the tracks. We've been told to leave the station while they take him away, the man, he jumped down shouting something we couldn't hear, like it was some kind of statement, some protest maybe.

The crowd on the stairs began to move towards the exit again, like passengers boarding a flight. He could see blue lights flashing when they reached street level.

The phone then showed the tattoo of an owl on the other girl's arm.

Amanda's owl, Emilia said.

A barn owl, with intense eyes staring out of a white face. Pointed ears and deep black eyes. The head of the owl swivelled around as she moved her shoulder to display the face. Black lines emanating from its head. Underneath, a slogan he was unable to read in that short space of time and may have contained the word sea.

The video turned back to Emilia, and she said, Have to go now, Dad. She blew him a kiss with her thumb. Another two or three thumb kisses in a row, and in that moment, she looked so much like her mother.

He thought of her suddenly growing up without him being present. Before he knew it, she would turn into an adult and he still felt she was a child. Wishing he could be there to collect her from school and bring her for an ice-cream on the way home, her favourite place, where they once left her scooter behind and he went back later to find it was still there. How happy they were playing Minecraft together.

His heart remained on the streets of Berlin after the phone call ended. He continued moving through canyons of apartment blocks and crossing bridges with railway tracks underneath. Across parks with plane trees where somebody had hammered bottle tops into the bark. Murals painted on gable walls. A community centre with the photograph of a woman in the window holding up a large black key. Graffiti showing up on the façades like some colourful pattern that grew in the minds of monks and began spreading across the city into every corner and every doorway. People walking in and out of paintings with designs that extended to their bodies in tattoos and other forms of body graffiti in ancient scripts. Streets with bikes chained up to railings and e-bikes abandoned and dealers from elsewhere fighting each other for company. People drinking bottles of beer outside late-night shops and people at the fast-food booth ordering *pommes frites*. Blue lights flashing outside the underground station. A crowd of people standing around, including his daughter and her friend Amanda with the owl tattoo, while paramedics in red uniforms and yellow stripes were coming up the stairs carrying black plastic bags with his own body parts inside.

Fourteen

In the car park of the hospital, as he sat waiting for his friend from Westport to be discharged, he heard a helicopter approaching overhead. He had the window open and he could hear it getting louder and louder as it began to descend. He was unable to see the helicopter and that increased the terror that came with such noise. It produced a storm in the car park. Leaves and dust began to blow around in a swirling gust and he was forced to close the window. People coming from the hospital to get back to their cars began looking up and covering their heads. A nurse in blue medical uniform arriving for work could be seen turning away and holding her hands over her eyes.

The helicopter flew very slowly overhead and he had the feeling it would descend on top of the car. It was the sound of war but obviously not war, he told himself to write in his journal, because it landed some twenty metres away on a circular landing pad that was painted with a large red cross.

They were delivering a patient to the hospital. Medical staff could be seen rushing towards the helicopter with a gurney. Once the blades stopped rotating and the engines began to calm down, the doors of the helicopter opened. The pilot and paramedics got out and went around to open a further door at the back so they could transfer the patient to the waiting gurney.

The injured person – was it a farming accident or an accident on the cliffs maybe? – seemed to be a woman. She was half sitting up, talking to the nursing team as she was being rushed away to the emergency department.

The sound of the helicopter and the war storm created in the car park triggered descriptions of war he had seen in movies and books. He didn't need to have been in a war situation himself to be able to feel the terror of it. Or maybe it evoked a subliminal, second-hand memory of war that he might have inherited from his parents, which they had inherited from their parents who had actually witnessed the bombing.

And just then his daughter forwarded another photo that didn't make a whole lot of sense. A group photo, this time, of factory workers standing around a consignment of products waiting to be shipped off. The workers looked like they had been called together for some kind of publicity photo where they said goodbye to the items they had manufactured.

The photo came with a caption – happy faces.

He had time sitting in the car outside the hospital to examine the photo.

The workers wore bright blue shirts and navy trousers. The shirts had two grey reflective bands going horizontally across the chest. Most of the workers were men, some of varying origins. Some women as well, wearing the same blue shirts with the reflective bands, others at the back in ordinary clothes, the office staff most likely. Some of the men had beards, long hair, glasses, a few wore navy caps, a nice bunch of people, you would have to say. A man in the front row had his arms crossed, one or two had their hands in their pockets, others with hands clasped in front of their private parts.

Other than that, he had no idea why he was being sent that image. Happy faces, so what? He had to text Emilia back to ask what it was about.

Then he received the message that his friend had been discharged. He got out of the car and walked past the grounded helicopter up to the main entrance. His friend from Westport stood outside with a broad smile. A stout man with a beard, wearing a light blue shirt and dark trousers, carrying a bag under his arm. He had a deep resonant voice and thin long fingers, which had been playing the piano since he was a child. He was free to go while others were being admitted. In that moment, it was clear to him that his friend, who had feared the worst and had now been given the thumbs-up, represented all the good things in the world.

Nothing calmed the sickness in his heart as much as the sight of his friend from Westport smiling with a bag of belongings packed for going home. He still had the plastic identity tag around his wrist that a nurse had attached when he was admitted. Perhaps he was leaving it on as a souvenir, to remind him that he now had his life back.

As they drove out of the car park, past the resting helicopter, his friend with the plastic bracelet on his wrist told him that in the ward where he had been staying there was a patient in the bed opposite who kept calling his wife darling. Ah, darling, the opposite patient kept saying to her. Darling, you're an angel. Darling, you're a darling. He had the bed by the window and the man opposite kept phoning his wife every hour to let her know that she was his darling. Darling, it's too much for you to do all that work in the garden alone. Don't be carrying those bags of mini-chip bark in from the car, wait till I get out, darling.

He must have called her darling at least a hundred times a day, so his friend told him.

Darling, listen, his friend heard him saying to his wife on the phone in the tragic voice of a boy, they're keeping me in for another night.

The opposite man sat on the bed in his clothes, so his friend said. He was ready to go home even though he was not allowed to go. He was heartbroken. As I was getting ready to leave, his friend said, we had a short discussion about the food at the hospital, and the opposite man gave me some parting advice. In a hushed and serious tone, like it was a secret he didn't want anyone else in the ward to hear, the opposite man mentioned a particular supermarket chain where they sold pre-prepared dinners for as little as six ninety-nine. All you had to do was reheat them. Beautiful. Turkey and ham, the opposite man said with a wink, was his absolute favourite. The best thing of all was when his wife went out and bought one of those pre-prepared meals as a surprise and got rid of the packaging and served it on a plate as if it was not bought ready-made in the shop and all he could say was – Ah, darling.

I had the impression that was her name, his friend said. She came to visit him twice a day, and as I got talking to her once, I was tempted to call her darling. When I was leaving, his friend went on to say, I went over to shake his hand and told him that I had a friend from Berlin outside waiting for me. Then I felt guilty about leaving him behind, so I told him he would be getting out soon. I had no authority to say that to him. Only this strange compulsion to make him feel better. He had tears in his eyes, he said, reminding me once more not to forget the ready-made turkey and ham dinner – beautiful.

It seemed, his friend said, as though hospitals not only saved people from pain and death, but also gave each patient some renewed clarity about their own existence. The person being discharged is not only given their health back and allowed to return to the streets for a period of extra time, they also receive a parting revelation. In this instance, it was the discovery that every man has an opposite man in his life. The man you might have been. The man who gets left behind while you walk away. The man, perhaps, that you have been doing your best to leave behind. Like there's two men in each man, the man you are and the man you keep walking away from.

His friend's name was Brian. He was more than a friend, a man he got to know well in Berlin and whose insight and stories he admired to the point where he sometimes liked to imitate his voice. A father figure, perhaps. He came originally from London and lived for a number of years in Berlin before he moved to Westport with his wife Gabi. A folk singer whose head was full of gallant sailors and beautiful maidens splitting a ring, one half each, so they would recognise each other when reunited. She was originally from Transylvania and came to Germany to study psychotherapy before they both settled on a piece of land in Westport where his parents were from. After graduating from university in Bucharest, she worked with a German company, translating for a sales team who sold chainsaws. She spent her time going into villages in the most outlying regions, demonstrating logging equipment. All those mountainy men watching her leaning down to start up a chainsaw and showing them how easy it was to cut down a tree. She hated the sound of chainsaws and ended up in Berlin where she studied psychotherapy and found a job in the role of career guidance counsellor. She had travelled to many places in South America in the meantime, studying alternative forms of therapy and healing.

My friend Brian, he wrote in his journal, is a good bit older, more like a father to me. Same age as my father would have been if he was still alive, but the opposite. Like an alternative father. A father without red dots on the wall.

I used to think that every man I met was a version of my father, he wrote. My father is still ever-present in my life. At any moment, he can appear without notice. In pubs and restaurants. Cafés. On trains. My father suddenly turns up with the red dots on a wall behind him. Sometimes, he wrote, I see the red dots first, like a precursor, and my father appears later. Other times, he appears briefly in the shape of another man and disappears again, leaving the red dots behind him. It might be described as a form of migraine, he wrote. The red dots appear and I know he's there, without fail. The map of red dots has become such a formidable part of my memory that I cannot recall my father without seeing them.

As they drove back from the hospital, he wished that his friend Brian was his real father. He could not help referring to him in his journal as a friend-father, my alternative father.

They caught sight every now and again of the holy mountain. It towered over the landscape in the shape of a triangular peak, not a cloud to be seen. He said to his friend that he had climbed the holy mountain with Katia when they were on their honeymoon, not because the mountain was holy but to see the surrounding landscape and the ocean. And when they got to the top, he told his friend with the identity tag still on his wrist, they were enveloped in a cloud and saw nothing. He planned to climb it again, he said, just to see what they had failed to see back then.

They came into the town and drove past the river, up to the street that went almost vertical and looked like a deck of cards with houses stacked up in different colours. Around by the square with the clock at the centre and out by one of the streets spinning away again. They arrived at the house where Brian lived with Gabi. She came out and left the door open to welcome them and to say thank you for collecting Brian at the hospital. They didn't own a car. They were gladly dependent on friends to bring them to the supermarket, or down to the bus station, otherwise they walked.

Their house was full of light. The first thing that struck me, he wrote, was the stained-glass panel situated at the top of the landing. It shone through the house like a piece of friendship. It was bought in Spain, Brian told me, and the Moorish design of blue and gold spread around the walls from early morning right into the late afternoon. It was like a clock, Brian said. It moves along the walls upstairs in the morning, then it gradually projects along the wooden floor of the bedroom, and finally, provided the sun is out, it comes down the stairs step by step into the hall, laid out in a Moorish mat just inside the door. He found himself standing for a moment in those liquid colours, he later wrote in his journal. Transformed by the blue and gold light across his face.

And perhaps the rush of elation he got as he entered the house and walked down the hallway was some kind of magnified homecoming. A welcome that made him feel like a child coming back after being away on his own for the first time. He was led into the kitchen and asked to sit at the table, a bunch of wildflowers in a jar, the back door open onto the gardens and the sound of birds. There was a basket of newly cropped potatoes by the door. He could see the garden fork stuck into the soil and he got the smell of baking in the room.

There was a Victoria sponge cake on the counter. It had two layers of jam inside. A welcome home cake. Gabi made tea and cut the cake, placing each slice on its side. And while she was pouring tea, she smiled and said, You haven't changed a bit, Lukas. She remembered a particular time when they went out on a lake near Berlin and got lost, when he and Brian had to take turns rowing because the engine failed and it was nightfall before they got back.

Fifteen

They asked him how things were going in Berlin and he could not avoid telling them about the break-up. He didn't want to say that his marriage was over. The word contained too much ending and perhaps there was still some hope left in his voice. They listened with their eyes as he told them that his marriage falling apart seemed to correspond with everything else that was falling apart in the world. Their eyes wanted more and he told them he had the feeling that all great love stories end in dissolution. In novels. In poetry. In break-up songs. Like the entire world had now become one big break-up song.

They smiled, because he said that with the touch of melancholic irony that was permitted to a man whose love story had so recently fallen apart. He could not avoid uttering a small inward laugh. It came on a surge of irrational emotion, which he later associated with the fact that there were two people sitting across the table from him listening. It gave me a powerful feeling of acceptance, he wrote. It brought me close to tears, to be in a room with my friend Brian and his wife Gabi and all their kindness. They gave me an overwhelming feeling of being heard.

He told them about the photo he had received earlier on from his daughter while he was waiting in the car outside the hospital. It was not much to look at, just a photo of some factory workers, so he didn't take out his phone to show it.

After tea and cake, with the door open and late-afternoon sun coming along the floor, after Gabi suggested going for a walk and said, Lukas, would you like to see the gardens and he said, Sure, I would love to see the gardens. After they left the plates on the table and stepped out into the sunshine. After they passed by a row of blackcurrant bushes and she said they got a crop of fourteen kilos this year, most of which they freeze for the winter and put in their porridge, and he said it was hard to believe you could get such a harvest from a couple of bushes, and she said with a smile that they were almost self-sustainable, pointing at a bank of solar panels on the roof of the house.

After they passed by a hazel tree, first planted when they arrived, Gabi said, with sunlight coming through the branches. The sun inside the tree, he later put in his journal. After they passed through a gateway of two large rocks into a further garden and came to a plot of leeks shooting up like individual fountains, he told them about the factory workers.

He didn't let them see the photo because people hate those people who take out their phones in the middle of a conversation to show some image or to prove some fact.

It seemed so uneventful. Just a group of factory workers with no context.

Happy faces.

The caption was what intrigued him. Workers standing in an interior dispatch zone around a consignment of products looking happy. Behind them, there was a lateral stainless-steel ventilator shaft. Some yellow boundary markings along the floor.

Happy faces, he said once more.

He left a pause. A philosophical pause that indicated how uncertain the word happy was.

The workers in the photo appeared to be … happy. Yeah. No, no. I mean. Happy.

He hesitated again.

Like … happy.

The word happy contained so many interpretations that two people could never agree on the same version. It could not be taken at face value. It could mean the opposite. It needed qualification. Happy to one person was everything missing to another.

Some of the workers are smiling openly, he began to explain, while others seem a little more internal, relaxed, content, quietly proud, as they stand in non-accidental rows for an official website shot, so it seemed. In one area, he told them, some men and women are laughing, maybe one of them made a joke prior to the photo being taken, while others, who have not heard the joke, are more serious. It's hard to know what they're thinking and what their hopes are in life, only that they seem to be happy.

Happy-in-the-workplace happy.

They look, he told them, from his own experience of working in factories long ago, like a family. He could remember as a student working in the dispatch area of a publishing house where that family atmosphere was encouraged by the management. Every Friday, before the end of the shift, he recalled, the foreman would put a crate of beer on one of the packing counters in a gesture of camaraderie. It became an accepted part of the working conditions and failing to put up a crate of beer would have been seen as a gesture of hostility. The crate of beer, in other words, held the family together.

Maybe that was the intention of the photograph in this case, to make the workers appear happy and proud to belong to a surrogate family, apart from their own families. Any underlying tensions, personality clashes, rivalries, political differences, even plain physical dislikes, of which there were many in the publishing house, he recalled, were suspended in the moment the photo was taken.

What struck him about the photo, apart from the fact that he had no idea why it was being sent to him, was how clean the place looked. You could eat off the floor, he thought, like you could eat off the floor of the publishing house where he had once felt he belonged to a family. Behind them, underneath the ventilation shaft, you saw a row of internal windows, obviously in use by the office staff and product designers, engineers, creatives, whatever they might be called.

What he failed to see, he told them, and what shocked him when his daughter texted him back to explain – Dad, you're such a dope – is that the workers were grouped around pallets laden with munitions.

I was looking at the faces, he said, not the products.

Standing upright on wooden pallets, he described to them, are rows of shining red-brown missiles. They look like bowling pins. Stacked in rows of four by two, held in place by green binding tape, with a flat board on top that allows the tip of each rocket to point out through individual holes, so you have, he said, eight red dots in each consignment.

Which, of course, he wrote in his journal but did not have any need to tell them, reminded him of the red dots that his father had on the wall of his office. The red dots created by the rocket tips protruding through the protective wooden casing had nothing whatsoever to do with the red dots on his father's wall, but he could not help thinking they did.

It was impossible to say where the rockets were destined to be deployed.

In war, obviously, Gabi said.

Brian entered the conversation, saying he had heard of investigations in which shrapnel from such a missile could be identified and traced back to its origins. It's not only by a serial number with which each missile is assigned but also by sound recordings. Audio experts are now able to reconstruct the trajectory of a rocket from clips gathered on mobile phones. The forensic science of ambient noise, he called it. Each sound examined by wavelength patterns to determine exactly where the missile came from.

Each missile was pledged to a particular destination. Each missile, Brian said, is built ostensibly for the purpose of self-defence and other ideals of self-preservation, armed with a precision-guidance system that could deliver its payload with great accuracy to within a metre or two of a selected target. Within the floor area of a bathroom, let's say, Brian said. It left very little room for error. Even less room for explanation after it had been delivered.

Gabi said she had read about a recent protest in which activists had attempted to block missiles being loaded onto ships destined for unspecified war zones. Could they have come from the plant in the photo sent by his daughter? It was impossible to know. In any case, she said, the shipment affected by the protest was only temporarily held up and the rockets eventually reached their intended destination.

It was unfair, he said to them, and they instantly agreed, to associate the workers pictured alongside the crates of brand-new, precision-guided missiles with any particular target. The workers could hardly be made responsible for military decision-making. It would be like saying that a woman who gives birth to a man with a gun is culpable for his actions. Or that washing-machines built by the same company that produced the rockets could be included under the same dividends as the profits of war.

He made sure to dispel any implied link between the workers and the results of their work by saying the rockets leaving the factory floor were as harmless as bowling pins. Their primary motivation in the construction of these missiles may have been the mission of bringing peace and happiness to areas of conflict around the world. It had nothing to do with the job satisfaction of workers in a munitions plant. Wrong to use the word happy, in this instance, to describe how they might feel.

They came to a greenhouse. The tomato plants inside seemed to be trying to grow out through the glass, like faces pressed up against a window. He rubbed some of the leaves with his thumb and pointing finger.

Scent of tomato leaves reminds me all the more of tomatoes than tomatoes do, he later wrote in his journal.

Scent of Katia.

He told them that the photo was significant for another reason. His daughter informed him that her mother had made the mistake of including the photo on Instagram without fully assessing the consequences. The photo, which could not be associated with any particular bombing raid, since each rocket is presumed innocent until proven guilty, had become part of the school investigation of the *Guernica* incident in Madrid. The image had been downloaded and posted by one of the students involved in the unfurling protest in front of the famous painting, making Katia even guiltier by association. Her approval, along with the photo of their daughter's larynx, had been picked up by one of the parents and was currently being used as part of a campaign to have her removed from her job as an art teacher.

She's being cancelled, he told them.

The photo was saying nothing that was not allowed to be said. It was just a bunch of factory workers. Only the comment – happy faces – was implying something that was not allowed to be said. And Katia's painting of her daughter's larynx as a statement about freedom of speech was another version of what was not allowed to be said. All of these things that she was not officially allowed to say as a teacher were giving parents at the school good reason to have her dismissed.

Sorry for loading all this on you, guys, he said.

Gabi turned to face him.

Are you OK?

I'm OK, he said.

Which was a clear admission, of course, that he was not OK. She inclined her head to one side with a smile and asked him the same question without words. He answered the question once more by looking away at a row of beehives without a word.

He felt the hand of his friend on his shoulder, even when there was no hand on his shoulder, only the sensation of trust.

The bees, earlier seen attracted to a bank of lavender bushes, were constantly flying back to their hives as though there was not enough time left in the day. The sun was beginning to sink but the light was still there in the sky. The midges were out in force. A blackbird went screeching across the ground in front of them. They could hear the sound of an open-air festival coming from the town, though it was impossible to make out the song that was being sung. And the bees. City of bees, he wrote. The hives, twenty in all, pointed towards the morning sun. He felt the power of all that industry.

Walking back to the house, they passed a cottage at the

edge of the land that had been painted white. The windows and the door were painted bright red in the traditional style of cottages in the West of Ireland. Brian said he built the cottage from rocks lying around the fields. It was designed initially as a fully soundproofed studio where he had, along with local musicians, recorded some great sessions.

I can't show you inside, Brian said. We have two people living there at the moment. A young mother and her son. Mira, the mother, is a great singer, he said. I've recorded a couple of songs with her both in her own language and in English. She's got a voice like nobody else around here. Her son Omar has just turned eighteen, but he's a bit troubled by the place they left behind. He's got a job in Supermac's for the moment. He's no idea what he wants to do with his life apart from going back to be a fighter. His mother is trying to give him a better future here but he seems determined to go back.

I've asked them to come over for dinner, Gabi added. You'll enjoy meeting them. It will be good for them to tell their story.

Sixteen

Over dinner, he had no urge to talk, only to keep listening and watching.

Mira and Omar arrived carrying various dishes they had prepared. Omar was very silent, wearing a hoodie down over his head. He was good at handling food. They placed the dishes on the table, then Mira explained them one by one. A dish of falafel along with a small bowl of sesame sauce that had a peppermint leaf floating on top. A dish of roasted aubergine mashed up with olive oil and lemon, with fronds of dill around the edge. Hummus. Tabbouleh. Lots of thin flat breads that smelt like they had just been heated against the side of a steel pan.

Omar spoke only with his hands.

As they sat at the table, Mira said to her son that he could take the hood down while they were eating – It's not going to rain inside the house. Omar looked up at her from the side and refused to take his hood down.

Gabi had made stuffed red peppers. Brian spoke about

the sauce that went along with them. It was quite simple, something he had once picked up from a friend in Berlin. You heated up some herbs and a little stock in a pan, he said, then you added lemon juice and rum and maple syrup, along with some thin slices of apple until they were soft and slightly caramelised.

All this felt to him, he wrote later, like he had entered a movie. The flow of words, the taste in his mouth, the faces and the smiles, even the sullen looks that Omar cast around the table without saying a word, were to him like part of a story in motion before his eyes.

Brian began talking about a time when he was nine and they sent him back from London to stay with his aunt in Mayo, not far from Westport. Small house with no heating. And guess what, Brian said, they brought in a lamb one day and slaughtered it right there in the kitchen on the stone floor.

Gabi said, Brian, why are you telling this?

Brian said he had been thinking about it when he was in hospital. I don't know what it was about the hospital that made me remember it. The lamb was on its back and four women holding the legs, the head hanging over the end of a bench, staring upside down at a picture of Our Lady. His aunt Moira stood with the knife in her hand waiting for one of the women to say go ahead. She stroked the lamb's head and said there was nothing to worry about, my love, this will be over in a moment. There were bowls all around the kitchen into which various parts of the lamb were placed as soon as they were cut up. And afterwards, when the women had cleared up and washed their hands and faces, they sat at the table smoking cigarettes and drinking a glass of whiskey and talking and singing.

It was like being sent home to a foreign country, Brian said. London to Mayo. A nine-year-old boy with a tiny suitcase and no idea where to go. The only thing that was familiar to me was the accent. I still get the smell of lamb sometimes, he said, a fatty smell like candle wax that got into my clothes.

Mira then spoke about how she witnessed the very same thing happening when she was a child, but it was in an apartment on the fifth floor.

My grandmother, Mira said, carried the lamb up in the elevator, holding it like a baby. They prayed and slaughtered the lamb on the kitchen floor with a towel over its eyes so it might not see the knife coming. People came dressed up in their best clothes to collect the parts and there was nothing left the next day, only that fatty smell, just like you said, Brian.

He was sitting on the same side of the table as Brian. On the far side were Mira and Omar, and Gabi sat at the end close to the door.

Mira began talking about the place that she and her son came from. She was speaking to her son in little bursts in their language, just to make him connect to the people around the table. She described a photo in which, she said, her mother sat with another twenty or so women on the back of a cart.

The poor horse, Mira said.

Omar was listening to everything.

Oh, my God, Mira said. Some of the women were making room for one or two more women at the last minute until the cart was literally so full, it was going to collapse under the weight of them all. The cart was built with rubber wheels, like a car, but still and all, she said, that poor horse had a big job getting it in motion, like it needed a push start.

Tell them, Omar suddenly said.

Yes, Mira said.

Tell them what happened.

She waved away her son's impatience and said the women were all working in the same place, making linen tablecloths and scarves and other items like wedding dresses, beautiful white dresses down to the floor that had to be embroidered and fitted with lace edging. They were on their way home from work and somebody thought of taking a photo of them on the back of the cart, like it was a miracle in motion.

Let me show you, Mira said.

She took out her phone and scrolled down for a moment while Gabi was sharing out strawberries into small bowls. She stuck a biscuit in each bowl, like a wheel had come off a cart.

Tell them, Omar said once more.

It was basically our form of public transport, Mira said. A horse-drawn bus that brought them there and back from work every day.

She passed around her phone. It went to Gabi first. Then it moved on around the table. The phone had a pink protective backing and the screen was cracked. When it came his way, he stared at the photo of the women sitting on the cart with their legs hanging down over the edge. They were sitting with their arms around each other, holding on, some waving, some talking over their shoulders, some holding shopping bags. One or two of the women wearing sunglasses because the evening sun was in their faces. Some of them laughing as the photo was being taken, while behind them, the road was full of cars and trucks and what looked like two men on a motorbike, one of them carrying a flat-screen TV.

That's my mother in the middle, she said. Her arm is around her sister.

He saw the two sisters on the cart. The image of the women together carried such optimism. It seemed like a moment when the world was at peace and no harm could come to them, smiling and holding on to each other, their legs dangling over the side like children.

Mira fell silent. She seemed to retreat into herself, back to where she came from. She was unable to say any more, something blocking the next thing she needed to say and didn't want to foist on this company around the table.

Omar stood up. He appeared to be about to speak for her but there was some white rage inside him that made it equally impossible for him to bring out the words. Like there was so much to say in one go and so much hurt in his mother's heart that he could not find the right place to start.

All of them, he said in a breathless voice.

He left those words in the air as if they explained everything. His mother's thoughts passed on without having to articulate them, the way sometimes a song can explain everything that's on your mind without any need to speak. Like there was a full speech to follow with the details included but no longer necessary because everyone around the table understood.

All of them in one strike, Omar said.

He stood at the table and looked at his mother.

They were all killed instantly.

Omar turned and left the room. Mira stood up to hide her crying. Gabi got up from the table and went around to hold her from behind. They stood in that powerful embrace with Gabi's arms wrapped around Mira's stomach, not letting go. Softly speaking with her face sideways against Mira's back, right into her lungs, saying, It's all right to be sad, it's all right to be afraid, it's all right to cry, we're here to cry with you.

Seventeen

When he was writing all this down in his journal, he could not remember the name of the pub they went to that night. It was such an uncommon name, not Murphy or Molloy. It was so non-obvious, so non-McCarthy or McNulty, it should have been easier to remember. He could have texted his friend to ask for the name of the pub. He could have left a blank space to be filled in later. He thought of looking it up online but that kind of retrospective research clashed with the true things he needed to keep. For the moment, he called it the yellow pub on the hill, halfway up the street from the clock tower, on the right, not far from where he parked the car on a steep incline. Where he took a photo of them on a crooked bench, no exaggeration, the bench was sloping down at a seasick angle.

It was completely reasonable, he wrote, even if it seemed funny to us, that the town council had, many years ago, bolted that steel bench into the pavement at such an absurd gradient. It was for people walking up the hill with their shopping to sit and catch their breath.

My friend Brian slid down the incline and Gabi came sliding down after him in a wide blue dress and her hair tied up on top. The photo shows them both squashed together by gravity at the lower end of the bench, both laughing and the house behind them perfectly straight.

In his journal, he could only remember thinking that the yellow exterior of the pub had somehow penetrated inside and left a golden glow on people's faces. Like the entire interior had been sprayed with fake tan, he wrote. Just in the door, there was a woman with golden arms holding a drink in her hand, laughing at something she had been told just before we arrived and I must have misjudged her age, she was younger than her laugh.

The place was packed, he wrote, and my friend Brian was immediately mobbed by people he knew. Welcoming him, embracing him, slapping his shoulder, offering him a drink as though he had just come back from the dead. I got introduced as the friend from Berlin. I was handed a pint of Guinness. I took a creamy sip and looked around at the shape of the pub. The owners had broken through into what was formerly the hallway of the house. At the back, they had extended into the kitchen where the musicians were set up in front of an old range, no longer in use, obviously. The range had a beige colour that went along in some coincidence with the yellow frontage of the bar and offered a place for them to put their drinks.

I had the impression, he wrote, that the bar was on an incline, but that's an illusion brought on by the angle of the street and the crooked bench, just as the golden glow across the faces was no more than a memory of looking through the orange-coloured objects that my mother kept when I was a child.

Somebody spoke to me, he wrote, and I didn't hear him with all the talking around me. Whoever it was may have spoken to me a second time and I thought it was somebody else he was talking to until I heard him mention Berlin, and by the time I turned around to answer, he had already given up trying to speak to me. He may have been one of the people I got talking to later on – we set aside the false start and he told me that he once lived in Berlin. He knew Brian while he was there and gave me the dates and the jobs where he worked including a printing firm where he said the noise of the machines was deafening.

At one point, he wrote, a woman put her arm around my waist and apologised instantly with a shriek when she discovered I was the wrong man, her husband was wearing the exact same jacket. I swear to God, she said, pulling her arm away as though she had touched a hot radiator. I had no idea how to respond, he wrote. I was too honest and glad not to say anything that might sound clever or cringing. The moment became even more awkward when I saw her reporting the mistake to her friends, pointing at me with her chin and saying, Don't all look at once, Jesus, and they all immediately looked.

He stood with Brian and Gabi in a small group at the bar while Mira went over to the musicians. Brian spoke about his time touring as a folk singer all over Europe and other parts of the world. He was once invited to take part in a festival in Brazil, in the city of Salvador. The drumming in that city was something else, he said. Drumming all day and all night. It was wonderful. No matter where you walked in that city, you heard somebody drumming, sometimes a group of drummers, either out in the open or in some hidden place inside, like they might have been underground and the drumming was coming up through the streets.

After the event, I was taken to a restaurant near the port, Brian said. In the old part of the city. It was a huge place, high roof, and floor-to-ceiling windows looking out onto the harbour. It must have been a converted warehouse, I thought, where they kept imported goods. You could see the yachts where the cargo ships were once at anchor and the lights reflected on the water. When I got the menu, I asked the man beside me what the place had been originally intended for, before it became a restaurant, so I was told quite openly that it used to be a holding centre for slaves.

You know, where they kept the slaves tied against the walls and sold them at auction, sometimes in lots chained to each other. All the evidence of that had been erased, Brian said. There was no plaque, nothing on the back of the menu or anywhere else to let customers know this had once been a human warehouse. I had to leave, Brian said. I couldn't sit there and have dinner in a place like that, thinking of the fear in their eyes, not knowing where they would be sent to or what was happening to their families and never going home again.

I ended up walking around the city, he said. All that drumming going on in the streets. People drumming to remember where they came from. Drumming across the ocean. Drumming all the way back to their land of origin.

That drumming is something I will never forget, his friend Brian said. It's right up there with any of the other great wonders of the world. I'd go back there any time for the drumming. Like there was some kind of unwritten law that the drumming had to be kept going at all costs, they could never allow a silence to break out, even a minute without drumming would amount to some great disappearance. Drumming is what kept them in existence. When somebody became exhausted after hours of drumming, a different drummer would step in until he had no more drumming power left in his hands and another drummer would take over, keeping the beat going right until dawn.

Bit like the Irish in London, Brian said. When I was growing up. My family and their friends kept singing songs to take them home. Back to where they came from. Somebody always had to be singing, downstairs after we were sent to bed. Singing in a pub, in the community hall, in a bus shelter, on the Underground. A man going home drunk and the song coming in the window at night when you were in bed looking up at the streetlight on the ceiling. A woman singing to a child as you passed by a house. A security man outside one of the department stores humming a song that everybody knew the words of. No matter what time of the day or night it was, no part of London was ever without a song, because silence was like being forgotten.

Singing to be remembered.

Drumming to stay alive.

Brian then went over to join Mira, and Gabi had another cherry nectar, the barman will know, she said. He wrote how he sometimes forgot that speaking to people in a bar was not like writing about them in his journal.

He watched Mira as she began to sing with Brian backing her on guitar. There was a tragic call at the back of her throat that was unique. Her voice reached the edge of a scream, full of dignity and despair, like she was singing from the ruins of a building that had been destroyed.

Gabi gave me some of the background, he wrote. Mira and her son Omar managed to get out, while her father stayed behind. They had still been in touch with her father until recently but they had lost contact with him now. He had been in military detention where, by some strange irony, he was safe, until he was released back into even greater danger in a place with no shelter. All they could do now was hope.

She summed up the conditions that Mira and her son had escaped from in one sentence – they're eating the soup and burying the dead with the same spoon.

Omar had been badly damaged by it all, Gabi said. He's become quite radical. Says he wants to go back and join the fight to free his people. Mira seems to have no way of stopping the rage building up in his head. She's afraid he's going to get killed. He's in touch online with all these people who want him to return. Mira, she said, thinks they might have booked him a flight, so he has obligated himself to go. He has the need to stand up for all those women on the cart, including his own grandmother.

Gabi said it was perhaps the people he talks to here who are urging him to go and fight. At school, at work, he kept meeting people who told him it's only right to fight for the freedom of his people. That's what the Irish did. That's how this country found its dignity. Fighting for its own independence. And you know what, Gabi said, it seems that he will never be accepted here until he goes back and achieves that same freedom for his own people. No matter how much he speaks with a Mayo accent and does all the things that everybody else does and joins in with other lads from work to have a drink and a smoke and go to hurling matches and whatever else, he will remain nothing more than a refugee until his people have their own place in the world.

Mira sang an old Irish emigration song. They were the best love songs, Gabi said, all that geographical distance. She said Brian had added a new verse to reflect the conditions that Mira and her son Omar had come from. Mira stood with her shoulders forward and opened with the words *A stór mo chroí*, which Gabi translated as treasure of my heart.

In the voice of a mother, or a lover, the song laments the departure of a loved one, most probably going off to America. Gabi explained how Irish people used to hold what became known as an American Wake, because the person leaving might as well be deceased. There's a well-known place in Donegal called the Bridge of Tears. *Droichead na ndeor*. She had been there with Brian once, she said. A stone bridge over a small river where people said goodbye. The families would walk up to that point with the person leaving, then watch them walk away out of sight before turning back. It was more like a funeral, they used to say, because the person gone away might never come back. The Irish for tears, she said, is *deora*. And the word for an emigrant is *deoraí* – tearful traveller. The song describes the person left behind calling for a speedy returning, as if they were even more out of place, more lonely, more homesick, than the person who went away.

In his journal, he wrote how her voice became a physical sensation. The words touched his arm. He put down the final verse, which Brian had added to the old song.

You will still hear the key, as it turns in the lock.
And the walls hold the welcome and laughter.
And the voice of a child in among the ruins,
Is softly and mournfully calling,
A stór, a stór, won't you come back soon,
To the ones who will always love you.

He remembered to put down that she repeated the chorus with a variation in the last line.

A stór, a stór, won't you come back soon,
To a land full of love and freedom.

On the next page, he wrote how he got back late and the headlights projected the magnified shape of the horse onto the side of a steel barn. The enormous outline of the horse, galloping backwards at great speed and slipping out of sight again. The woman of the house still had her light on, so he decided, as he was pulling into the car park, to switch off the headlights. Out of courtesy, he didn't want to shine the lights straight into her room. He got out of the car and closed the door quietly, then stepped inside and stood looking at the portrait of the writer in the hallway.

With the emigration song in his head, he could not help remembering what the writer had once said about the twentieth century. When this century receives its name, the writer with the black beret said, it will be called the century of the expelled. Which was, of course, exactly what he would be saying right now in the twenty-first century if he was still alive.

The century of refugees.

The writer spoke with his lower lip and didn't take the cigarette out of his mouth. A soft irony that was touched as much by sadness as it was by humour and accusation. The dispossessed. The displaced. The stateless. The voiceless. The century of no coming back soon.

Eighteen

As he stood by the door, before he turned to pick up the key to his room, he saw the surfers coming along the hallway. They didn't switch on the light. They spoke in whispers. Full of misdemeanour. They were dressed in bathrobes, most of them. Some of the men wore nothing but bath towels around their waists. The girl with the aquamarine eyes – Taylor he remembered to call her – came at the end of the line, also wearing a towel, which she held closed at the front with casual confidence, in one fist. Her eyes, he would write, were luminous. Like they were never switched off, even at night. Powered by some photovoltaic energy gathered during the day and allowed to shine in the dark.

While the others had already opened the door and stepped outside, she stopped to stand in front of him, her eyes almost too bright to look at.

We're going night swimming, she said.

Sounds good.

Come on, Lukas. You'll love it.

The towel left her shoulders uncovered and he could see a design of tattoos in various colours. The image on her right shoulder appeared to be a bunch of exotic grapes, blue and pink, that might have been harvested on some distant planet, dripping down to the top of her breast. A tropical place of abundance. On her right arm, some ancient lettering that held the code to her mind.

A man with hairy legs and a rain mac for a bathing robe held the door for her, a contradiction of seasons.

You can swim, can't you?

Of course, he said.

Come on, then.

She tried to link his arm with her free arm, the one with the ancient script, but he then held back and said he had to go to his room first.

Give me a minute.

She disappeared and he walked back along the corridor to his room. By the time he switched on the bedside lamp, he saw the surfers going past his window on their way to the beach. Some of them had already dropped their bathrobes and towels, running through the gate that normally kept the sheep from coming in along the beach to try and get into the garden and eat all the plants, so the woman of the house told him. The driveway was built with a cow filter set into the ground, a series of horizontal bars that kept the sheep out as well. Another thing he bore in mind when he was arriving back in the car that night, the clatter of polls made while crossing, so he remembered not only to switch his headlights off but also to drive in at a speed that made no returning noise.

He saw Taylor outside his window and her eyes became a Virgin Mary nightlight as she gestured for him to hurry up. He waved back and she went running ahead, throwing her towel onto the side of the gate.

It was bright enough to see the shape of her white body in motion, full of animal speed. He was moved by an intensely primitive desire to run after her. Like he wanted to catch up with her and bring her back right away. He would let her into his room through the window so that she didn't have to go around the long way, through the front door, past the writer with his twentieth-century conscience.

He watched them running into the waves. The night was calm and the sea was full of invitation. And as he saw them swimming with the stars out, he became strangely inert. He could already foresee the empirical experience of the woman with tattoos pulling him into the water in a ferocious dash. He could see himself carrying her on his back, laughing as they fall under the waves. He could see all the way into this bright new partnership of joy and sexual adventure, holding her white body, the tattooed arms, the script of her thoughts, the bounce of her breasts, staring into her phosphorescent eyes.

Why was he such a non-participant?

Here was his chance to join them. The immortals. The community of happiness. The country of now and lightness and devotion to fun. Instead, he remained in the district of thought. The duty to put everything into words. He could not get the happy workers and the pallets of rockets out of his head. He kept thinking of the women on the back of the cart and how such a tragic event might be reversed. It was hard to go night swimming while his mind was still trying to put the women back on the cart again with their legs swinging. He sat down on the bed and opened his journal. In capital letters at the top of the page he began with a single word.

TRAJECTORY.

He described everything being turned around. Time moving backwards. Experts on the ground wearing white helmets and white gloves picking up pieces of shrapnel. He saw them placing the twisted scraps of metal into plastic bags and numbering them, like a crime scene. He saw them talking to eyewitnesses and gathering audio information from mobile phones. The see-through bags with the pieces of shrapnel being taken away to a laboratory where they are assembled into a missile. The restored missile on a table with all the available information in a blue folder, named and dated and tagged. The direction of flight and the time of delivery. The experts track the missile back to the fighter jet from which it was fired, then all the way back to the airfield, the storage bay, the crates on which it had been transported with the name of the manufacturers. The reassembled missile taken away to be kept in a safe place along with the blue folder containing the provenance details.

He wrote about the trajectory of the missile making its long journey back to the plant where it was made. Transported on a truck that is heavily guarded. Each part of the journey documented and signed off by logistics teams with meticulous security. The shipment is held up along the way in a seaport by protesters, but then allowed to continue. The transport is monitored by helicopters, integrating with normal traffic along busy routes back to the small town where the missile was originally produced. Back to the factory floor where the workers stand around pallets laden with products that look like bowling pins, wrapped in green binding. The collegial atmosphere, some smiling, some not. The workers finishing at the end of the day, changing out of their overalls back into civilian clothes. Getting into cars and driving out past the gate with the name of the plant boldly written in stone, set into a landscaped lawn with a few medium trees. Some of them go for a drink together, others go for a run or some alternative sporting activity.

One or two of them picking up some last-minute items at the supermarket. Others go straight home to their families where the children talk about their day, what went right and what went wrong, some minor injustice that needs to be corrected, holding the child close until the tears of the day are wiped away, before they sit down for dinner and the TV is on in another room showing football. Some of the bars in the town stay open late. The main shopping street is deserted. The rubbish bins are out, waiting to be collected at first light. The homeless people under the bridge. The clock on the market square is gone past midnight and the town is asleep.

He heard them coming back from the beach. He heard their feet slapping along the hallway. He heard them talking in the room next door. A man saying something in a deep voice. A woman laughing. Music came on and he could make out the track that was being played. Water running and water switched off again. A knock, maybe an elbow banging against the wall. He opened the window. There was salt on the glass, the scent of seaweed in the air and the hush of waves spreading out on the sand. He climbed out the window and crossed the boundary wall draped with old fishing nets and walked down to the shoreline.

Nineteen

He told the sea that he was waiting for Katia. When she comes, he said, we will walk up to the deserted village together. He wanted Katia to wear her green jacket and her cheeks to be red from the wind and a bit of rain in her hair.

They would walk up to the deserted village in the afternoon and see it coming to life. The ruins would no longer be ruins, but a collection of homes with the roofs attached and the smoke rising. We would see the children on the road playing, he said to the sea. The dogs would come out to bark and welcome us. We would come into the deserted village no longer deserted but full of people busy carrying things on their backs and women standing at the edge of the road talking and men coming up from the sea and a young woman in a doorway with a naked child on her arm. The children would be shy and hide behind their mothers. The mothers would be shy of her clothes and her hair. They would cautiously come close and ask to touch her jacket and feel the fabric of her skirt and stroke her hair with their fingers. They would be talking in a language that we don't understand, asking questions, wanting to know where she got these beautiful clothes. The schoolteacher in the village would be called to translate. A crowd would have gathered on the road with everybody talking about her shoes and what shoemaker designed them. A child would give her a white stone and she would give her back a coin that was both precious and useless in a place with no shops. Boys would start running up and down the road in their bare feet for no reason at all but the excitement at the arrival of strangers. The men holding back at the entrance of the village smoking their pipes.

One of the men, an older man in his seventies but still looking like a boy of seven, would put the fishing gear he is carrying down on the ground and stand back to look at her, wondering where he had seen her before and if she was famous. He would say that he knew she was coming by the way the sea was acting that day. A curl in the waves that was unusual. Then he would step forward and take off his cap and shake her hand. He would tell her it might be a good night for turbot fishing, and if he was a younger man and she wasn't already married, she might not rule him out with all his knowledge of the sea. Then he would yelp and stamp his foot on the ground for her.

The old people, sitting on the stone sofa at the gable end

of a house, speaking a continuous narration about visitors from another world.

She would be brought inside one of the houses and made to sit down at a table. The mother of the house would make tea and put a plate and a knife in front of her and she could not refuse to eat what she was given. All the people of the village wished for was to see a stranger eat and sip the strong tea. She would cut the scone and spread some butter that came straight from a churn, along with some jam made of blackberries. They would watch it going up to her mouth and she would get the taste of it with the entire village now looking in the window. She would have to let the mother who made the scone know, through the translator, that she had never before tasted anything like it anywhere in the world and they would want to know where she had been, had she ever been in Paris?

She would allow the mother of the house to try on her shoes, but that only made her blush and give them back, they were too good to wear in a village like this. And with the sun going down, after consulting with the schoolteacher and the other women at the door, the mother of the house would say it was too late to send anyone back out on the roads. It would be agreed among the women, old and young, who ran the village and made all the decisions, that the visitors had to stay the night. Everybody living in the house would go and sleep elsewhere so the bed at the end of the room with all the smoke inside would be free now with clean sheets brought from the house next door and an extra pillow made of goose down from another house and everybody all the way to the end of the village would be saying the visitors were staying overnight. They must be staying overnight. Yes, they're staying overnight.

Everything about her would be repeated a hundred times. And when the sun was gone and the light was fading and they lit a candle, one of the women from the far end of the village would come to sing a song, the lament of three Marys, which would be translated in a whisper. Then a bottle would be produced with a clear liquid inside that would be first poured into cups laid out on the table and then passed around to the people outside until everybody, man and woman of all ages, had had a sip from the neck. A man would come with a tin whistle to play a tune accompanied by the clicking of spoons and somebody drumming hands on the door. And the woman of the house would ask her to dance across the stone floor with hands entwined and hair flying at the back, her shoes making such a confident clack that people outside who could not get a look in would be talking about it for years, the sound of foreign shoes on the floor.

When it was time to sleep, the women of the village would carry in a steel basin and fill it with hot water so she could have a bath after coming all the way from Berlin and Paris. The basin would be standing in the middle of the stone floor with the village still looking in the window until the schoolteacher finally told everyone to go home and the door was closed. She would hang her clothes up on the kitchen chair and get into the bath and use the small bar of soap that came from another house at the entrance to the village, sent up wrapped in a cloth and carried by a young girl with long hair like it was the most precious item ever seen and even the tiniest scent of it was something stolen.

The village would lie down at last and the silence would be like nothing ever heard before. The candle was put out and the stone walls of the house held the glow of the fire. The village was going to sleep. The last words were spoken and the last pipe was heard knocking against the wall and put away in the pocket of a jacket. The darkness would be so profound and infinite, reaching all the way into the universe. The stars would be out and the night descending on the village would be accompanied by a chorus of minute sounds. Nothing but the purest ingredients of silence. The cough of a child. The sound of a lullaby. The hoot of an owl. The stream running along the road and the whisper of people in their beds in a language that sounded like water running. A warm breeze coming in through the windowless window across her face and the sea keeping time.

Twenty

The surfers were already gone out by the time he was up. They were making their way down to the beach in their wetsuits. Dark slender figures from a different planet, indistinguishable from each other, heading to another elated encounter with the waves. The woman of the house was clearing up the tables after them and she told him to take his time, you just keep writing down your thoughts, Lukas, before they all go missing in your head.

The day was bright and blue, good for walking, he wrote. He could sense that the woman of the house was waiting for him to finish so she could have a quick chat. Like she needed to make sure he was not one of the night swimmers and needed to pick the right moment to verify that. He thought of showing her the photo of his friends on the crooked bench as evidence of where he had been the night before and that he was in a yellow pub he could not remember the name of and he had only had one pint of Guinness and heard a great song about emigration that ended with the words come back soon.

Then he got another call. He sat with his head bowed over the breakfast table, speaking quietly into his teacup so as not to be overheard. The woman of the house did her best not to listen, even though she could not understand a word of what he was saying. She could read from his crouched position, from his frown, from his way of smiling politely as if there was nothing wrong, that he was talking to his wife in Berlin.

He told Katia that he was doing fine. What does that mean, when a man tells his former wife that he's doing a lot of walking?

The bog is on fire, he said to her.

He described how there was smoke to be seen all around the island, like a blue veil. It didn't come from any of the houses, it was some unseen fire spreading underground that was impossible to stop. There are no flames, he told her, just a general smouldering below the earth and smoke seeping up through the peat like there's some enormous furnace down there. There has been no rain for a while now and the fire is just going its own way.

It's Emi, she said.

She wanted him to take an interest in his daughter. Instead of all that walking across the bogs, he should be looking out for Emilia, who had now, in case he didn't already know, joined the gang of protesters who had unfurled the poster in front of the *Guernica* painting in Madrid.

The woman of the house passed by with a stack of plates and a fork fell on the floor beside him, which she leaned down to pick up.

Emilia has begun to hang out with one of the student protesters, Katia said, I don't know what kind of relationship she's getting into. It's the one covered in tattoos, who posted the photo of the munitions factory.

The woman of the house said, Excuse me.

You need to talk to her, Lukas, as a father, Katia said.

What can I say?

She was arrested, Katia said. Yesterday. By the police. Your daughter, Lukas.

Arrested. For what?

She was taken into custody at a street protest on Hermannplatz. I had to go down to the police station with her documents to prove that she was only sixteen. Then she was finally released with a caution.

The woman of the house went back into the kitchen.

Are you not worried?

Of course, I'm worried, he said.

You need to do something instead of wandering around in the past out there in the West of Ireland. This is happening now. This is the present, Lukas. And Emilia hanging out with that crowd is not helping my situation with the school tribunal.

What am I supposed to do?

He found himself virtually addressing this to the woman of the house as she came back into the room.

I'm not going to tell my daughter who she can get into a relationship with. It might be just pure friendship. And so what if it isn't?

The woman of the house looked as though she wanted to have a quick word with his wife and set her straight.

He listened to another lengthy speech coming from Berlin and smiled once more at the woman of the house to let her know that everything was fine, just a small issue with their daughter, you know, the usual – teenager stuff.

While the woman of the house was making noise at the far end of the room, he began telling Katia that he was not going to curtail his daughter's decisions.

You took a photograph of her larynx, he said. You made a painting of her voice. You encouraged her to speak out, which is a good thing, Katia. Whatever it is that motivates her, whether it's the arms industry or the climate catastrophe, it's best to let her find her feet. It's her future.

The woman of the house was creating a flapping noise with a tea towel that sounded like applause.

She's right to make herself heard, he said to Katia.

While the woman of the house was slapping more and more crumbs off the tables, he brought the call to an abrupt end, with a burst of anger that was not really like him at all, the woman of the house would have said.

Give her the freedom to speak with her own mouth.

The call ended with no kisses.

He put the phone down on the table and stared out at the surfers. The breakfast room was silent. If the woman of the house had any doubt before, it was now abundantly clear to her that he was a man alone. He was not allowed to be alone. It was not a country that allowed people to be alone. It was her duty to stop him being alone.

She pushed some chairs back into position, then came to stand over him. He assumed that she was waiting for him to finish so that she could flap the crumbs off his table and bring in the Hoover.

I'm in the way now, he said.

Why would you think that? she said with a smile. A guest could never be in the way.

He sometimes felt, for no particular reason other than the memory of his father looking at him as a child, that he was in the wrong place.

Be in the way, she said.

Thanks, he said, that's very kind of you.

He got ready to leave, but she pressed her hand on his shoulder so he could not move.

Stay there as long as you like, she said. Take all the time in the world. Let me know if there is anything you need, I'm just making a couple of scones.

She grabbed an empty plate and signalled that she was about to let him carry on writing his journal, but then she lingered a while longer to ask him if he drove all the way back from Westport with no lights on.

The question confused him.

She told him it was none of her business what time people got in but, Lukas, look, there was really no need to drive into the car park with the headlights off, trying not to wake me. It wouldn't wake me because I was awake already, reading my book, and the headlights shining into my room at night is not something that would ever disturb me.

My own two boys are grown up now. They're gone to live in Dublin and New York. One is a solicitor and one is in start-ups, whatever that is.

So don't be trying to arrive back with the lights off out of consideration, she said, because I'm only too happy to hear my guests coming back.

He nodded.

Just one thing, she added. Please, if you don't mind, remember to give the front door a good bang when you come in, to keep the sand out.

He apologised for leaving the door open. It was easier

to own up to that much instead of explaining what really went on the night before.

She said her husband, the man of the house, had suggested installing one of those self-closing devices on the door, like they have in the pharmacy. The door opens outwards for a good reason, she explained, so the wind doesn't push it in. Some guests, she said, think they've been locked out, until they realise they need to pull instead of push.

He said he would remember to close the front door properly in future.

She was against the idea of a self-closing device because it seemed a little unwelcoming and awkward for people with suitcases who might end up fighting with the door as they came in and the wind will normally do just that in any case, she said. Sure, isn't the wind the best self-closing device you can get, only last night there was no wind.

He was not the type of person who left doors open. He was, in fact, a man who hated leaving doors open and made sure doors were always closed. An open door felt to him like part of himself was exposed to the world.

As a joke, he said he might get lessons in how to close a door properly.

The woman of the house laughed and slapped him gently on the back of the head like a boy.

Don't trouble your mind, Lukas, she said, it was probably one of the surfers.

He heard her in the kitchen, then closed up his journal and went back to his room to get his sunglasses and his cap. It was a fine day and he had so much to say to the sea.

The surfers had already taken over the beach close to the guesthouse. The sea was calm with perfectly formed waves rising and falling. Each bulging wave came from the deep, timed to follow the one before in a continuous sequence. He stood watching the surfers. Black shapes that looked more like dolphins than ever. He admired their superior skills of well-being. He envied their viability. Swimming out on their bellies and jumping up on their boards in magical expressions of fun. It was time for him to move on. What he had on his mind could only be said to the sea alone, so he walked to the furthest tip of the island, to the forgotten beach. Where the sea looked more primordial. Where the laws of life and desire were formulated a billion years back, where we crawled out on land at the beginning of time and became us.

Twenty-One

He placed his shoes on the sand. They were pointed towards the sea, a light pair of blue runners with white soles. He took his sunglasses off and put them in the pocket of his jacket. He folded up his jacket and laid it on top of the shoes in a neat rectangle with the arms crossed over and the collar facing up like a shop display. He put his trousers on top of the jacket and his shirt on top of the trousers in the order of a man going to bed. His cap went down last with the phone cradled inside.

He walked to the edge of the sea. There was nobody around, only the mountain behind him. He walked into the water with the waves gradually rising up to his chest. He didn't feel the cold, only the fight in his arms against the enormous volume of water. He swam out and said to the sea that he could not help feeling responsible for the harm in the world. It was his nature to take things to heart. Some duty he had inherited from his father to hold the outrage in his journal.

He could not lose sight of the women on the back of the horse-drawn truck. They were part of his life now and he could hear the sound of the missile descending before the women even had time to look up and say, That's for us. He imagined things not happening. He imagined things un-transpired, damage undone, people unharmed, lives brought back from the dead, houses and schools standing up out of the rubble, the missile being reconstructed from scraps of metal picked up by officials in hazmat suits and returned to the manufacturers, like a faulty product on a pallet of harmless bowling pins.

The sea held him above the waves and said, What is it with you guys?

We had a man here a couple of months ago who folded his clothes in that same arrangement of departure. Did the woman of the house not tell you? He gave himself into the water in the same place, so intentional and thoughtful, a man like yourself, full of fucked-up things in his head, leaving that same neat stack of clothes with the phone on top, no note. Normally they go in off the cliffs fully dressed and we hand them back after nine days with no eyes and no lips.

He told the sea how his mother used to remind him not to bite his fingernails. Every time she saw his hand going up to his mouth, she would say, Luki, stop biting your nails. At school he would bite them in secret, and when he got home, she would pick up one of his hands and smile and shake her head, Luki, you've been biting your nails again. Then she was suddenly gone and there was nobody to tell him to stop. After the funeral, he said to the sea, he could remember thinking that he was free to bite his nails as much as he wished because his father was never bothered about that kind of thing. Once his mother was no longer present, he had to make all those decisions for himself. He was alone and it was his own choice to stop biting his nails. Just as it was now his choice to swim and stay alive.

Out there on the water, he soon realised that the sea had the upper hand. Staying above water became a struggle. The voice of the sea kept urging him to release control. While his arms were pounding on the surface, he felt an emotional release in which he was confronted with an urgent, suffocating range of feelings that he seldom experienced on land.

He lost sense of time. Not slow time or fast time, but more like the entire collapse of time. A clarity opened up in his mind that was not unlike the delirium he felt when he was sick with chest infections as a boy. That terrifying liberation from the faithful surroundings of the known world into a place with no gravity, no feeling of individual identity, only the overwhelming sense of weightlessness.

He was back in the peppermint-green house and saw his father coming to visit him. He didn't want to see his father, only his mother. There was something in his father's eyes that seemed to concur with his own, like they both missed her so much, they could not bear to meet each other's gaze. His father embraced him and he could feel the pencils in his top pocket leaving an imprint on his cheek. The smell of his father's shaving cream and the fear of never going home again.

As he drifted further out and entered this battle with the waves, he heard the voice of his mother.

Luki, I'm coming to collect you.

It took time for him to realise that he was speaking out loud in German, but it was the voice of his mother he heard coming from his mouth.

I'll be there soon.

Bin bald da, Luki.

Right in close to his ear, her voice took up the entire ocean, repeating the same words over and over – I'm coming to collect you now, Luki.

He saw the path leading up to the house with the peppermint-green façade. The roses on either side. The dark green door and the avenue of thorns big as knives and the strong scent of mulch. Again and again, that same walk along the path with the roses, the weakness in his legs, gripping her hand and not letting go.

He had entered into a beautiful incoherence.

He was all ages at once, man and boy, released by a false

sense of security in which he felt he was being embraced from behind. Lured into letting go. Into not being afraid. His mother holding him in a powerful hug that felt like he was back on land. Her voice entering into his back, Everything is going to be fine, Luki. I'm holding you and you're safe.

He must have swallowed some sea water. The taste of cold soup with too much salt, gagging at the back of his throat. The nauseous weight of it sloshing around inside. He could no longer trust himself to stay afloat. Everything began to swirl and turn. Everything duplicated in multiple waves to the point where he was no longer in control of his own direction.

He craved the safety of land and the solid assurance of the earth beneath his feet. A land creature out of place. He became lightheaded. Inspired by visions of wonder. By the feathery shape of ferns. By the spiralled coils of shells. By the colour of grasses and the sheen of silver in trees. By the flight patterns of birds and the astronomical design left behind in all things with the rotation of the earth and the pull of the moon. He imagined rocks aligned in cycles of fertility. Mountains with human hearts. Trees with faces, covered in cloaks of green moss. Broad rocks with eyes of white lichen watching him from the coast without a word. And the sea kept rolling the waves.

Let go. Let go.

His mother came to collect him. She was wearing a white blouse with blue buttons. Her shoes made a sound on the wooden floor that could belong to no other woman in the world. She held his hand as they walked back out along the path with the screaming roses and the smell of mulch and small tags stuck in the earth with the individual varieties named. They came to the gate with the metal squeak. His mother closed it behind them and he could remember thinking they were not walking away fast enough. They had to wait for the bus and she gave him a sweet from her handbag and told him that everything was fine, the results at the hospital were good, she would never have to go away again, she was not going to leave him.

They got home and she gave him a toy car that she had bought for him. His father was jealous because he was allowed to sleep with his mother, so that she could sing all the songs she brought with her from elsewhere in her language. And he wanted, while he turned to swim on his back for a while looking up at the sky and the vast ocean underneath, to do nothing but listen to the songs and fall asleep.

He was unprepared for such joy. His ribcage was open and it felt as though the water was getting inside and his heart was going to float away. A delicate thing with no weight, bobbing on the surface. Like one of the tinted, blown-glass objects that his mother kept in a locked cabinet when he was a boy. Deer and wild boar and other forest creatures that she collected to replace what she had lost when she came from elsewhere. He was allowed to hold them only while she handed them to him one at a time, whenever he was coughing and had to stay home from school. She carefully put them back into the vitrine each time. They disappeared after she died, just one of them he remembered keeping in his room, a tiny horse that glowed like an orange moon when it was held up to the light.

Twenty-Two

By then he had already gone beyond the measure of his own powers. The sun was in his eyes. The land seemed out of reach. Behind him was the mountain where he and Katia once lay on the grass with the engine parts of a crashed plane around them. Grey pieces of engineering that would never be subsumed into the earth. Wind whistling in the hollows. Doomed voices of men shouting while trying to adjust the altitude at the last minute before they hit the mountain. On a foggy morning so close to safety. A few feet higher would have saved them.

He was like one of those doomed voices now. His clothes on the beach had become a small parcel of mortal value, a clue left behind to be identified by the woman of the house along with the remark that he didn't bring a towel. There was a sign up in the bathrooms asking guests not to take bath towels to the beach, please, but still and all, she would say, he went without a towel and left his clothes folded like the last fellow. God bless him, the woman of the house would be saying. His body and his clothes sent back to his poor family.

Don't taunt me, the sea said, in a squall across the surface that drew him further out. We have so many involuntary ones now, the sea added, the unprepared, the people in search of a better life, drowned even before they set sail, in vessels built of faith and optimism.

He felt the might of the tide against him now, pulling and pushing at will. He was running with no foothold, threading in a foreign dimension in which the miracle of flotation was not unconditional. His breathing full of doubt. Swimming in his own tears. The ballast of despair in his limbs. Still longing for the living world and its earthly rescues, not yet ready to be taken down in that unequal contest with the ocean.

He said to the sea that he had spoken to Katia and there was no love in her voice.

The shore was drifting away. A distant territory that no longer held any tangible meaning. He was hyperventilating with the effort to make it back to the point where he had entered the water, already seeing the land as a human fabrication, a collection of stories full of random images such as the reflection on a steel teapot and the woman of the house counting towels and a grey horse in a field. He heard drumming and voices talking and children laughing.

He heard the sound of an ambulance siren. He heard the voice on the underground telling people to stand back, the doors were closing.

He tried to hold on to those irrelevant details to stay afloat. A head full of distracted associations, bobbing on the surface like a buoyancy float.

Let's see how good you are, then.

The tide had already pulled him away to another part of the bay, deeper than the bridges of Berlin with the railway tracks calling from below. Far from where his small pile of clothes stood in a column of unhurried disappearance. There was nobody calling him back, no friend or next of kin, nobody waiting for him to refill his shoes.

Come under, the sea began saying. Come under.

His arms and legs no longer had the power to match the waves and the woman of the house would be wishing he had brought one of her towels after all. It's the surfers she had the problem with because they came back with towels full of sand and she had to shake them out and give them a rinse before putting them in the washing-machine. A man alone should never go anywhere near that forgotten beach without a towel.

Seriously, he said, trying to negotiate with the sea at this point.

The parents at the school were now accusing Katia of saying things that were not allowed to be said. She had, on the school trip, allowed herself to point to the *Guernica* horse and speak to the students about things that were not allowed to be said. That their daughter was now hanging out with protesters has made things even more difficult, he said to the sea, because it was now virtually impossible for Katia to claim that she said no such thing.

The choppy waves made him swallow more and more sea water. It went up through his nose and down the back of his throat, like the peppermint taste of fear.

Some of her students, he pleaded with the sea, have gone in front of the tribunal to give evidence that while she was pointing at the *Guernica* horse, she said, or at least hinted at, what was not allowed to be said by a schoolteacher at the same time as the poster was being unfurled. The poster with those exact words in the colour of blood. The words that nobody at the tribunal could even get themselves to say.

A cloud blocked the sun. The mountain became a dark shoulder, turned away, indifferent. Two gulls hovered overhead for a moment to see if he was a seal or a human, did he have any bits of fish to discard.

What can she do? he said, as the tide continued to pull him in the direction of the rocks. All this stuff that is now being said about her on social media, which she cannot refute.

The world has no time for denials.

Last summer, he said to the sea, as if the memory of happy times might give him the right to return to land. When we were still together, he said, a bunch of friends were up there in a cottage by one of the lakes outside Berlin. The owners built a lovely tree house around two enormous pine trees. The sap was on a bench and it left sticky marks on Katia's dress when she sat down. They went out on the lake for the afternoon in canoes, himself and Katia in a canoe that was marked with Native American designs. And Katia kept complaining about the sticky sap, like glue on her body, she had to keep pulling at her dress. Everybody around the table at the back of the cottage later on with the sun going down and the smoke of charcoal in the air and the food laid out. Could he remember it now to save his life – a beetroot dish, a bowl of courgettes marinated in vinegar and dill, a diced-up carrot and apple salad, and what else? Barbecued chicken and pork, he recalled, asparagus tips in rolled-up rugs of bacon and lots of wine. Katia brought a basket with lemon cake.

And the dog, he said to the sea, coming up underneath the table between his legs so he jumped as though he was under attack and the fork with the lemon cake flew out of his hand. The conversation at some point turned to athletics and gender issues and how much testosterone a competitive female swimmer was allowed to have. As well as other subjects such as East and West and how people were voting. And what was Katia meant to do, get all her friends to testify in front of the tribunal that they talked about nothing but sport and politics and they had never heard her say anything that was even remotely close to what was not allowed to be said?

He was thrashing more than swimming. Determined against the odds to get back to the shore and put all this down in his journal.

Come under.

Come under and be saved from all this human trouble. Come down into the deep and leave all the fucked-up things of the above world behind. Come and live with the family of the deep with nothing forbidden.

This whole thing with the school tribunal made him think of the writer in the foyer of the guesthouse with the black beret. Nothing had changed since the time he was alive and writing about silence and bread and lovers who speak about bread and lovers who can't utter the word bread to each other.

He wrote a book about a woman being cancelled.

A small book he had read at school. A piece of living fiction in which the writer described in the style of a police report, with all the times and dates meticulously included, what happened to himself in the guise of a woman whose apartment was raided by the police. At a party, she meets a man and invites him back for the night and he turns out to be a suspected criminal. By the time the police arrive in the morning, her one-night lover has already disappeared and she is taken into custody.

The writer's home was raided by the police. He was ostracised in his own community. He couldn't get a plumber. Waiters refused to serve him in restaurants. One Sunday afternoon, his home was surrounded by sharpshooters in a radius of five kilometres and the police found nothing when they entered the house but a couple of people having coffee and cake. The strange thing was, he recalled being told when he was at school, a police spokesperson had already informed the media, so the raid was reported in the papers a day before it actually happened.

The writer had the last word in literature. A book about a woman being deliberately targeted and cancelled by the media. Photographs of her appear in the newspapers in which she's made to look like a terrorist, a frightened expression that is converted by implication into a criminal scowl. He could remember the debates in school around a woman's right to choose whatever lover she wanted without being labelled an accomplice. That ancient witchcraft notion of female sexuality as a threat to public order.

Come under.

Come down to the floor of the ocean where everything is laid out in a stately reception room of crawling things.

Come down for the banquet of banquets in the dark with unseen eyes to welcome you.

He was begging the sea to show mercy.

Dear deep blue deep of the deepest deep and scuttling things along the floor. She's being cancelled for pointing at a horse with a spear for a tongue. All she said was, Look at the pain in that screaming horse.

Be reasonable, he said to the sea.

Come under, we're waiting for you. Be safe with us in the deep.

He was not ready to give up. There was too much going on in the world to let go. He began dreaming up ways in which he could burst into the tribunal and put the school board in its place, tell them how absurd and restricted their thinking was. How similar this form of repression was to all the repression in the past when the writer's house was raided and he wrote his book about a woman being cancelled. He imagined swimming into the board room with the jury of teachers and parents sitting behind a table with their bottles of mineral water lined up neatly. Reminding them of what the founder of the school had said in Nazi times about freedom of expression.

They had no idea what freedom was, he was begging the sea, apart from the choices between versions of almond milk, roasted or not roasted, with or without added sugar. Half almond and half oat. And what would you expect with the clothes they wore – a man in jeans and pointed leather shoes, a woman wearing a crinkled handmade scarf in bright green, another woman with hair chopped off at the back of the head thinking she was really cool from behind? One of the men with a surf rising over his forehead. An older man wearing a tie and a ponytail to signify that he belonged to the generation of remorse and guilt that broke with the past.

He kept his eyes on the shore.

I swear, he said to the sea, she described them to me in detail with all their conforming eccentricities. Mobile phones on the table to check the latest absurd rumours so they can turn her into a terrorist like the woman in the novel.

With all the water in his lungs, he imagined rushing into that board room and saying all the things that were not allowed to be said. He would see their shocked faces, because they needed to be on the right side of history and not even be accused of having heard what was not allowed to be said about *Guernica* then and *Guernica* now.

He imagined rushing forward to overturn the table with the bottles of mineral water and grabbing Katia by the hand, running out through the school corridors laughing. Out through the yard into the street. Running all the way to the Underground still laughing. Getting back together with her in one heroic act of survival.

There was a man standing on the strand.

The sun came back out and turned the figure into a silhouette. He could not recognise who it was. Standing completely still, not waving, not calling, not getting ready to help, merely observing his solitary struggle with the sea.

A last bid for survival seemed so pointless now and he had no more strength left in his arms and legs to rejoin the living.

Come below, the sea whispered. Leave all your land-based thinking behind and join us in the pelagic fathoms. Stop being so attached to the land. Stop owning the earth. Stop tearing it up in pieces of territorial property and private rights and places defended by walls. Be free of all that nationalism. Be part of a place where all voices are heard. This free and fluid continent of music. The untamed democracy of art. Come down and belong to that great song of the sea.

The tide had brought him right over to the rocky coast. He attempted to get back to the sandy part but his knee hit one of the hidden rocks underneath the surface. He hardly felt the pain, just the humiliation, like the injury was more personal with no blood to be seen. His hand came up red. His elbow and the toes of his right foot also grazed one of those unseen objects moving underneath him, like a shoal of fish made of basement rock. Creatures from the pre-Cambrian era lurking below with stone heads and stone backs. Boulder sharks with razor fins. Underwater birds with serrated beaks. Urchins with hairy spikes and crustaceans with amethyst claws waiting to get his eyes.

The man continued watching.

Lukas swallowed more peppermint water and felt overpowered by fear and failure. The dominance of the waves kept pushing him towards the rocky coast and pulling him back out again like an item of pollution, flipped around like a plastic water bottle and left undelivered. With the power drained from his limbs, he became so light in his mind that he could no longer think of anything but surrender.

Twenty-Three

He opened his eyes and saw that the man standing on the shore was his father. He had been dead many years, but he had come back now to watch over him. Perhaps he had waded into the water to drag him out on land at the last minute.

The sea was murmuring, like the voice of a crowd.

He tried to crawl away, but the fight for survival with the sea had left him quite deranged. He was unable to protect himself from his memory. In that moment, with the breeze coming across the beach on his back and his father towering over him, so commanding and silent, he did not have the strength to resist the things he had managed to suppress so far in his life. I was unable to cry when my mother died, he said to the sea, coughing up the salt water. At her funeral, I went around telling people that she was dead. My mother is dead, I told them, but I didn't really understand that she was gone. I saw the coffin but I still thought she would be back. I saw her coffin drifting away into the flames at the crematorium and the curtains slowly closing. I wanted to go with her into the flames. The curtains took for ever to close and the song that came over the speakers was my mother's favourite song about a place in America called Mendocino.

I didn't know how to be sad. I didn't know how to feel the music. It was only when I saw my older brother crying that I felt obliged to do the same. I cried not because she was dead but because I thought I would be sent back to stay in the house with the peppermint-green façade.

His father cast a shadow across his face.

With the sea speaking in a gathering of voices and the waves bequeathing and recouping in a slow rhythm, he could no longer hold back that time after his mother died. He was living alone in the house with his brother and his father. There was nothing in his life but the grief in his father's head. Nobody laughed. They watched a movie together from time to time, though they didn't like comedy, only action movies with lots of chasing. He remembered that his father brushed his teeth with a book in his hand. His father kept his mother's toothbrush in a glass in the bathroom. And also he noticed that his father could only put on his coat with the right arm first, not the left arm. The same way that he put his shoes on, right foot and then left foot. A practice he must have inherited from his father without noticing, until that moment as he lay on the strand puking up gushes of peppermint-green slime the same colour as the house he feared most in the world.

In a fevered delirium he experienced when he was nine years of age and suffered from breathing problems, he looked up at his father in a restless state, fearful, weak in his legs, flinching at any information that might emerge.

The tide was receding and the waves no longer reached his feet. His father stood over him, blocking the sun, staring down in silence.

That day in my father's office, he spoke to the sea, I was having a look around. I saw the map on the wall with the red dots and could not work out what they signified. I knew they had something to do with his work, but I could not help associating them with my mother's death and the cough I developed around that time, which had me in bed unable to go to school.

On his father's desk, he now recalled. with the wind across his back, was a black and white photograph of a machine that looked like a cement mixer, maybe a wood-pulping machine. The photo was grainy and he could not be completely certain, but he remembered some men feeding something into an opening at the top of the machine that looked like a human body. The body was naked. It was impossible to say whether it was a man or a woman. The body was lifeless, going in head first, so it appeared to him that the men were doing the job of undertakers.

Then I found my father standing right behind me, he said to the sea.

His father's eyes, he said, were not angry, more disappointed, the same solemn expression of regret that he bore when he told him that his mother had died. His father reached over and turned the photograph upside down but the image could not be unseen. How can you give back something you should not have witnessed at the age of nine? he later wrote. His father had no alternative but to explain. He sat him down and looked into his eyes, then began to tell him what was going on in the photo. It was a machine for erasing memory. The person who was being put into the machine was already dead and the people in charge were responsible for making sure he would disappear and remain forgotten.

The sea began whispering the names of the people underground. Slowly, each name was pronounced in a long, hypnotic roll-call of the dead.

When he became an adult, he read about this official Nazi programme. Set up to eliminate all evidence of mass graves. After his father died and he got a chance to go through his papers, he found the details of this erasure meticulously researched with all the available sources notated. A study that brought acclaim to his father as a professor dealing with German history. The map of red dots had been drawn up by the SS under the leadership of a man named Paul

Blobel, whose responsibility it was to dispose of all traces of mass killings. A photo showed Blobel with a long beard, not unlike people in rural parts of the east where he was active during the war. He had previously belonged to a special division, 4 A, involved in many of the killings in the first instance. That placed him in an ideal position to locate mass graves and eliminate them from the map. A man in charge of covering the tracks, in other words, undoing his own work.

In keeping with the secretive nature of the operation and the fundamental principle of erasure, this Nazi programme was not officially named, or even numbered.

Blobel was tried and executed for his crimes around five years after the war. While in custody, he made a long typed-out statement with his entire biography, how he came from the town of Solingen, famous for its knives, how he studied to become an architect. He was not very successful in his chosen career and became an alcoholic. He found his calling when he joined the SS, and though he was not among the top tier of officers, he was proud to be given the job of cleaning up the landscape. At his trial, he did not dispute the existence of red dots and mass graves, only the numbers. He felt the prosecution had overestimated the total number of dead and they didn't tally with his own figures, which were considerably lower.

Reading about the red-dot crimes as an adult did

nothing to alter the memory of when he was a boy in his father's study. The shock of this information, no matter how benevolently his father spoke to him in an unhurried voice, was like a punch in the stomach that kept coming for the rest of his life.

He could recall his father pointing at the map on the wall. The map was part of a curriculum in a school that had been set up by the Nazis to train officers in the most efficient ways of eradicating history. The classrooms were like ordinary classrooms, only the student officers were taught to forget instead of remember. They received special training in how to find and dispose of people who were buried in red-dot locations.

The school for killing memory, his father called it.

The people in the mass graves had been previously murdered, so the assignment given to the officers in the school for killing dead people was to make sure they could not be brought back to life in memory. The officers were given the opportunity to practise on bodies that had recently been killed but not yet erased. Once they graduated, it was their task to supervise teams of undertakers who would eliminate all traces of the human body either with pulping machines or by erecting large bonfires on which the bodies were burned, close to where they were originally laid to rest. The previously murdered people had to be exhumed and turned into ashes and tiny bone fragments before they could be reinterred. Over time, the earth would be restored to its original undisturbed condition, mostly in forests and other isolated areas of scenic beauty where there would be no point in relatives who might have survived trying to visit them.

The waves continued slowly listing the names of the people underground. The succession of names was accompanied by a murmuring in which the dead could be heard talking and calling to each other. Names that were being added to the list brought shocked cries from some of the names already announced. The parade of names and the murmuring of the dead became louder and louder until the entire ocean became a single voice of missing and mourning.

In order to completely eliminate any memory of those names, he now recalled his father telling him, to make sure, in other words, that the previously murdered people were twice murdered to the point of vanishing from the earth for ever, with no physical trace left, and no names to be remembered, the people chosen to carry out the job of re-killing them had to be killed in turn. Teams selected by force to carry out the exhumations would ultimately join the twice-murdered people so they would not be able to remember them either. In effect, his father explained, they were carrying out an impossible task of re-murdering the dead and then having to be murdered and re-murdered themselves. Until the last witness to all that memory was himself erased.

The very last man to remember, his father said, would not only have to kill himself but also re-kill himself after he was dead, so that no evidence could be found. Which proves that no atrocity can ever be concealed, his father told him. There will always be some tiny splinter of memory left alive. His father said he was trying to stop the memory of those places disappearing. And some day soon, his father said, he would bring them to see one of those red-dot locations where his mother had come from. It would be like going home to where she was born.

The boy who he was back then found it hard to breathe with the red dots in his chest. His breathing was audible and his father once brought him into a café to buy him a glass of hot chocolate. They sat facing each other at the table. His father smiled and told him to take his time. But he began coughing and they had to leave before the hot chocolate was finished because everybody in the café was looking at them and moving away, afraid of being infected by the red dots.

His father then brought him to a stationery shop and bought him his first journal. It had a light green cover with a white band across the front, he now recalled, where he could put his name and address and his age, along with the words above in capital letters – private, do not read. His father also bought him a fountain pen. Then he taught him how to put his fears into the journal.

He remembered bringing the journal home and writing about the people underground in one of those places marked by red dots. They were dead but they were afraid of being found and re-killed and made to disappear completely. He wrote how in his dream he went down underground to visit them, just to let them know that they were safe and the students in the school for killing memory would never find them.

In his first journal as a boy, he described how he met beneath the earth a girl and her mother who were doing their best to stay as quiet as possible. Whispering and trying not to laugh. They wanted badly to laugh at something they had been told before they got killed, only that it might attract the attention of people combing through the country looking for red-dot locations that were not yet erased from the map.

In that first journal with the green cover and his name on the outside along with his age, nine, he was able to assure the people underground that the re-killers were lost and the map of red dots had bigger red dots that were more important to find. The people he dreamed about were happy to hear that. The girl and her mother started laughing, even though they could not remember what was funny.

They told him, he wrote in that first journal, that their entire village was living underground and they could feel the heat of the sun pulling the crops up out of the earth. They could see great highways of mycelium leading through the ground and connecting up the roots of trees. A million crawling things were rearranging the earth to make it airy and light for seeds to find places to germinate. They could hear the footsteps of a fox lightly threading across the ceiling. They could hear crows as loud as a parliament in session. They found items of value that people in the village had buried in haste, reunited with their owners at last.

They were keeping their voices down, he wrote in his boyish handwriting, pretending it was just a field with nothing underneath only for the baker who decided every morning at the break of day to practise his trumpet. Letting people know that the bread was out of the oven. For God's sake, the mother kept saying, he was surely going to give them all away and there was no need to play his trumpet, everybody could smell the fresh bread in the air. He told them in his dream that they had nothing to worry about. He wrote, in that journal of a nine-year-old boy, how he assured them they would never be found, only by one man who came once a year in May to lay flowers in a field full of flowers, a professor of history in Berlin who is my dad.

His father disappeared.

The sea was calm and silent. He looked at the view in front of him, a stationary ocean, an unending space with a silver sheen across the surface. The curve of the beach and the bay enclosed by the cliffs on either side now held a kind of beauty that he had never known before. The rocks on to which he had been driven by the tide seemed so harmless now and it was as though you had to be nearly drowned to appreciate what it was like to be alive. Or maybe he had taken this beauty for granted, like all beautiful things in the world were there to help you forget what made you lonely. The sandhoppers were out, jumping around him in a dance that could only be described as joyful. Some sheep had come down to the grassy banks at the edge of the beach and they seemed to be unaware of how intensely scenic this place was, chewing in a kind of nonchalant unknowing. Sanderlings flew across the water and they had the knack of disappearing in flight, their brown wings making them invisible until they changed the angle of direction and the flock of white bellies underneath came into view again.

He got to his feet and walked into the water to wash the blood from his knee. The other injuries were superficial. He washed his face and stood with his back to the sea, closing his eyes and taking the heat of the sun like a gulp of hot food into his chest to gather his strength.

He made his way back to where he had left his pile of clothes. He put his clothes on in reverse order, his right arm into his shirt first before the left arm. The same with his trousers and jacket and his shoes, right first then left, and maybe there was more of his father in him than he acknowledged.

He put his cap on and took his sunglasses out, then put his phone away into the pocket of his jacket.

I sat down, he would later write, making sure that moment of survival did not go unrecorded. The sea was so deep and so blue, so silvery on top that I wanted, for no reason that I could think of, to do nothing but cry. Was I crying because I had survived? Or was it because I had met my father so long after he was dead and he wanted me to be safe?

There was no other reason for me to be so extremely happy and sad at the same time, he later wrote, now that I had recovered that memory. It was after that event in my father's office that I found out how to cry, he wrote. I cried every night, so my father had to get into bed beside me. We slept together, until the red dots in my lungs began to go away.

A car arrived on the road leading to the beach. Doors banging and voices approaching from behind. A family came down and the children ran from one end to the other, like a point-to-point race. The mother brought a basket and began unpacking lunch on a blanket she had spread out on the sand.

The shore became the seaside.

The family was joined shortly after that by a group of cyclists who came speeding down the hill as if they were going to freewheel right into the ocean, breaking through a large canvas to enter the view. They stopped and laid their bikes down sideways on the grass.

In his journal he wrote this.

Blue sea with white lace edging. Peace of mind I have never known before. Maybe I am ready for the future, now that I have found something good in my father, now that I owe him my life, my survival.

He walked along the road and looked back at the family sitting on the rug having their lunch. The cyclists were walking along the strand with the legs of cyclists. There was a seal in the water, its head over the surface like a buoyancy float. A cormorant went underwater and he waited to see where it would come up again, but it surfaced far closer to the shore than he guessed.

He continued walking with the sea on the right-hand side. The road was hot and shimmering in the heat. The flaming red fuchsia bushes began to block his view and he began to feel that he was the adult now, he wrote in his journal, and my own father had become a boy for me to look after. The past becomes childish over time and you're so much more grown-up than people were back then, making strange decisions that had no logic to them. Like the world will never grow up and they will be looking back at us wandering in a helpless state.

I thought of my father in his office, he wrote, not very good at dealing with children. He was not a violent man, only violent with information. I want to console him now, he wrote, even though he's been dead for years. I want to let him know that everything will be fine. We all miss her, my mother, but she's probably smiling right now, looking back at us and thinking of her son turning into the father of his own father.

He imagined fathers and sons going all the way back in history. A long line of men with the same names and the same faces, some regressing, some improving on each other, some standing still, some passing on their anger and some passing on their love, some passing on their intellects and some passing on their looks, some of them doing no more than replacing each other with the same jokes and the same stories and the same football team.

Twenty-Four

A cloud of smoke hung over the landscape that afternoon. It turned the road blue and hid the village from view. The cliffs that normally turned red in the evening had now become scarcely visible and there was a sweet smell of turf everywhere. Out of the smoke came the couple on the motorbike. She was waving once more as they passed by and disappeared back into the smoke again as though they had gone into the ocean.

The fire brigade was out. Two tenders sent from Westport. One of them had already run out of water and was sent back to pick up more from the lake. The firefighters were spraying out in the open and it was a bit ironic, perhaps, to be watering the bog. They would never find the fire. It was like searching for a rabbit gone underground, so the woman of the house said. You wouldn't know where it might come up next and start laughing behind your back. They might as well be hosing the bog with a water pistol, that fire is migrating under their feet, like an enemy without a face.

On the way back, he saw a man on the shore collecting bits of debris that the sea had delivered from the deep. A retired schoolteacher who was known to collect all kinds of things to keep in a shed at the back of his house. Perhaps he was not unlike himself keeping things stored in his journal. A collector of useless memorabilia, finding things along the shore that had nothing in them but the measure of time. A strange gallery, so he had been told by the woman of the house, full of objects that were of no use to anyone. Like a rusted wheel. Bits of wood and bits of plastic. Pieces of blue rope. An aluminium float. A slab of reinforced concrete with twisted steel rods emerging like black worms. A copper bowl that was bashed up by the waves. A wire mesh. A frying-pan with the handle missing. An old hairdryer. A plastic chair that might have come from a cruise ship and somebody possibly threw overboard.

He was known as the shore-ranger.

Everybody on the island appeared to have a title, it seemed. Along with their given names, each person had a more descriptive pseudonym. The shore-ranger. The Germans on the motorbike. The writer with the black beret. The boy whose horse ran into the sea. The mothers outside the shop. The returning emigrant. The Romanians. The Amazon man. The surfers. The surfers from Canada. The surfers from last year. The wild swimmer. The woman with the aquamarine eyes. The bog walker. The missing tourist.

The wild Atlantic driver. The person who comes for a day and doesn't stay.

Soon, he would have his own title. Your man from Berlin. The journal keeper. The archivist. The wild walker. The man without his wife and daughter. The man who talks to the sea.

The limping man.

When he got back to the guesthouse, the woman of the house was instantly alarmed. She said he looked shaken. What happened to him?

Lukas, she said. You're like a walking ghost coming out of the smoke. Look at your hand.

It's only a scratch, he said, trying to hide it. Must have grazed it on the rocks.

Let me have a look, she said.

He showed her his hand with the knuckles red and opened up. She took it in hers as though he was one of her own sons and said something would have to be done about it. She pulled him into the living room where the TV was that nobody ever watched and made him sit down while she went off to get the first-aid kit.

My God, she said, when she returned with a small basin of water and the first-aid box under her arm, I can't trust you out the door, Lukas.

She placed the basin on a small table and began to clean the blood off his hand.

Were you in wild swimming?

He nodded and she looked even more worried, as though she and the sea were sisters and they swapped all the news. It made her omniscient, and she had already been told that he nearly drowned up there at the forgotten beach. He was lucky to be alive, unlike the last man to have gone up there without a towel and hit the rocks.

The woman of the house put some disinfectant on his hand and bandaged it up. Then she said he would have to have some tea and a scone to recover. Oh, my God, she said, you look like somebody who has come back from the dead, Lukas, your wife should be here now to see the state you're in. Does she know that you go wild swimming?

He said he wouldn't want to worry her.

The woman of the house then stood up and she could see instantly that the knee of his trousers was darkened with a deep stain of blood.

Look at your knee, she said.

He tried to get up and let her know that he was going to have a quick shower, it was all fine, just a small bump, but she pushed him back down into the seat and said, You stay right there. Do you have another pair of trousers?

I do, yes, he said.

Because, she said, she had lots of clothes belonging to her eldest son who was around his size.

No, I have a pair, he said.

Take those off, right now, she said.

There was no option for him but to surrender himself into the role of a patient. He had been turned into one of her sons, their photographs were propped up on the mantelpiece, both of them receiving degrees at university. One of them looked like the woman of the house and the older boy looked more like the man of the house outside sweeping away the sand.

He took off his shoes first, the blue runners, right and left, then his trousers, right and left in the same order, slowly edging the fabric over the knee.

She examined the bloody knee, then began washing it with water until the basin went red. Then she spotted that his elbow was also injured, so she told him to get his jacket and shirt off as well. She began to wash and dress the wounds thoroughly, drying them off with a facecloth. She laid a piece of disinfected gauze on his knee, then strapped it with a tape going all the way around the back of his knee, shaking her head in disbelief, saying he looked like somebody just back from a war zone. She did the same with his elbow, then slapped his good leg and said, How is that? He thanked her and said she was so kind.

She gathered up his trousers and his shirt, then stood up and looked at him like a child unfinished.

She marched off with the clothes and he stood in the television room with the bandages around his knee and his elbow and his hand, looking at the photos of her two sons. The room smelt of disinfectant, like a field hospital. He heard the radio on in the kitchen and he made out the song that was playing, an old country standard with a gravelly voice singing a line that had the word fool and the word heart in it. Two of the surfers came in and briefly caught sight of him standing in the middle of the room and the woman of the house came back with clean clothes for him. The man of the house passed by outside and, for a moment, his face appeared at the window, squinting as if he was trying to read some fine print on the glass. The woman of the house paid no attention to him and handed over the clean clothes. She turned away for a moment while he got dressed.

Thanks, he said. I think I'll be fine now.

You're not fine at all, she said. Wild swimming without a towel. I could have given you a big beach towel if only you had asked me, Lukas.

You're very good.

You'll have to recover, she said, before I let you out of the house again.

She told him to sit down and not move an inch, while she picked up the bloodied basin and the first-aid box. He sat down and waited. Her sons were staring at him. Her husband was outside passing back and forth with a bucket. More surfers passed by going through the hall, just as the woman of the house came back with a tray, laden with tea and a scone and jam. And maybe the surfers felt left out as she poured tea into a cup from her own private collection. He was like a special visitor, like one of her own sons just arrived back after a long time away. The guesthouse was transformed into a home and she couldn't take her eyes off him. She sat on a small chair, just looking at his face and saying, Lucky you didn't knock your head, Lukas. That might have been the end of you.

And while he was eating the scone, he began telling her what she had already been told by the sea, her sister the sea, her big sister with long white waves, that she was right to treat him like one of her own sons because his mother died when he was a boy and his father was a professor of history who became obsessed with emptiness.

He gave his life to the study of memory, he said.

I knew it, she said.

It seemed, while she listened to him and reached over briefly to stroke his head, she already knew that his father had left a deep shadow on his life.

I didn't understand him, he said. He lived in his own head, always reading, never had much time to talk to me. He was not a violent man, by any means, he told her, only a bit rough with information.

And that's what made you go wild swimming like a mad horse, she said.

The woman of the house then told him that she never

saw much of her own father. He was working over in England, so he only came home at Christmas. And my mother, she said, the woman of the house before I became the woman of the house, kept everything going while he was away. When my father arrived back on a visit, it was like a stranger coming into the house and we were all shy of him. Nobody knew what to say and he didn't either. He brought us back sweets from England that we had never seen before. He smiled and I remember him picking my mother up in the kitchen and swinging her around until she said, Let me down, John, before I turn to butter.

Then my father was gone again, she said.

I remember once, my mother bringing me up to the phone box on my birthday so I could talk to my father and let him say happy birthday to me and tell me that I was a big girl, just like my mother, and already nine years of age.

That phone box, she said, pointing away out the window, outside the pharmacy, that used to be the busiest place on the entire island every Friday night. Look at it now, she said, it's a thing of the past, grass growing around the base and glass panels, some of them broken, all kinds of names and love hearts scratched into the black box where we used to put the money in, and no receiver, just the loose wire hanging down. That phone box was the only connection to the outside world and now it's no more than a toilet, the smell would knock you out.

There used to be queue outside that telephone box on a Friday night, she said.

All the women waiting for their husbands to call from a pub somewhere over in England for a couple of minutes, just to hear their voices. To let them know everything was good and maybe to pass on the latest gossip, like a storm had knocked down a tree near the football field and who was going over and who was coming back and sometimes a son might only meet his father for the first time on a building site, she said.

And you know what, Lukas, I never realised how lonely my father might have been over there without us, living in small digs at the top of a house with the smell of soup. My mother brought me up to make the call to him, putting the coins into the slot one night when it was raining. My father spoke to her for a moment and then she handed me the phone, but I heard nothing, she said. The line went dead and all I could hear was the crackle and the rain falling.

And when he finally came home for good, she said, he threw his suitcase out onto the waves. That was the custom here, still is, she said, for the returning emigrant to announce that they were home by throwing the empty suitcase out onto the ocean. She described it as a gesture of ending. The ritual of homecoming. Some of them turned it into a formal ceremony, a small speech, a couple of words, maybe nothing more than something muttered, maybe a roar at the sea while they flung the suitcase out and went up to the pub afterwards to drink like it was Christmas and prove to themselves as much as everyone else that the suitcase could never be used again. Her father brought her to the beach the day after he came back and they stood on the shore while he listed off the names of the cities where the suitcase had been. The suitcase, she remembered, was made of cardboard, reinforced with leather corners that were bashed by all the travel. It had lots of scratches and old chalk numbers that were faded. There was a belt tied around the outside because the lock that kept it closed was broken. She could remember him packing that suitcase with such a great silence in the house, taking it down from the top of the wardrobe and putting in his clothes, his shirts and his shaving gear. He had tears in his eyes, she said, that day on the strand after he came home, swinging the suitcase back and forth for a moment and then letting it go, out across the water. She said they watched it floating for a while as the waves took it away and it began to fill up with water, listing a bit and finally sinking out of sight. Taking away all those lonely years, she said, and all the time that was wasted in bars, all the heart-breaking phone calls, all that leaving and arriving and departing and never arriving. No more waiting for letters. No more packing and unpacking. No more going away and never coming back.

Twenty-Five

It was a bright day and he needed his sunglasses. Everything was so hyper-vivid, so newly invented that he felt like a child. The colour of the sky might have been digitally enhanced. The volume of bees was amplified to the buzz of an aircraft. The stone walls spoke in a language he could not understand and the landscape was as if seen through one of those 3D viewfinders he had as a boy within reach of his hand.

His heart was so wide open that a bird might come and peck at it.

The horse was there in the field, lying on the grass. He watched it standing up again. This appeared to happen in four different stages, all part of the same continuous movement – the horse raised its head, rolled forward on to its belly, hopped on to the front legs and finally pulled the entire body up on its hind legs. It brought to mind some kind of self-assembling outdoor furniture that would have come with numbered instructions and diagrams. A grey piece of upholstering that is laid out flat with legs stretched along the ground and inflated with a simple mechanism of inner springs. It was an ingenious design that transformed a collapsed hulk of bedding into a standing horse. The bandages around the injuries had been removed. The horse seemed to have recovered and maybe didn't remember what it was that sent it running into the sea.

He headed into Westport again.

He got another call from his daughter and stopped by a field and switched off the music. The field was full of cows. Black and white cows all facing the same direction, tails swinging. Designed in some digital formation, a battalion moving across slowly from right to left in obedience to algorithms beyond their control. Eating the grass in a systematic programme that was part of a predestined plan that would end up in hamburgers. Grass into black and white cattle into meat into happy moments.

Emilia was sitting with her mother in a café and said there was some good news. She would let her mother give him the details but there was something she wanted to say beforehand.

Just want to tell you this, Dad.

His daughter spoke with unusual enthusiasm, telling him that she had been on the U-Bahn just now and that she had seen a man he might have known.

I saw him, she said.

Who?

The guy with the pink jacket.

Knocked me off my feet to hear that, he wrote later in his journal. Suicide artist comes back to life. Wanted to be there to embrace her. She had seen the man with the voice from elsewhere and he managed to stay alive after all.

Tall guy, his daughter said. Wearing a pink furry jacket, like it wasn't his, more like a bomber jacket that was meant for somebody my age.

No shirt, Emilia continued. No socks. Just these flat slip-on shoes with the heels pressed down.

He listened to her account of the man with the pink jacket as though he himself had been found alive on the underground. As if by coincidence, his own survival in the sea corresponded in some magical way with the man on the train, both of them saved and ready to go on.

He's not very nice, Emilia said. Grumpy sort of guy. Wouldn't say thank you. Said people didn't care and he was going to throw himself off a bridge. Somebody in the carriage laughed and the guy in the pink jacket said, Oh, you can laugh all you like, just you wait, wait till you see.

Not many people gave him money, she said. Most of them were on their phones and took no notice of him at all. He got off at the next stop.

Where?

I can't remember, she said. It was not the stop where we saw the human incident. Not the station with all the posters of running shoes.

He even mentioned the name of the bridge, Emilia said. But I don't think anybody believed him.

Was it the Langenscheidt bridge?

Yes, that's the one.

She passed the phone over to her mother. The good news was that the tribunal had reinstated her with full pay. After all that, Katia said, and her voice was full of joy this time. Imagine, Lukas. There was not enough evidence to warrant dismissal.

He listened to Katia describing how she had sat in front of the school board, fully expecting her job to be terminated, when a member of the school board made a big speech on her behalf. All about how it was such a waste of time. She had no case to answer. That minor incident in front of the *Guernica* painting was irrelevant in the scheme of things. Nothing more than a distraction from the real issues. The school-board member went on to say it was crazy for them to be worrying about the past being compared to the present when there were far more pressing matters for the board to be concerned with right now. Such as the ratio of migrants that were taking over the classrooms. Here we are, the man on the school board said, worrying about a student protest in the Reine Sofia

Gallery in Madrid when our classrooms are overflowing with migrants.

Do you really want your job back now? he wanted to say to her, but he kept that to himself.

Congratulations, he said. I'm so happy to hear that you've been reinstated. It was completely unjust of them to have put you through all this.

She said she felt ashamed to be exonerated with that kind of argument, like nobody had learned anything from the past and the protest in front of the *Guernica* painting was in vain. Pointing at the screaming horse and connecting it up with the present day seemed to have come to nothing when this man spoke of classrooms filled with migrants fleeing from *Guernica* in our time. The man used the word re-migration. Bring back the Berlin Wall, the man kept saying. He's a parent from the former East, she said, and he kept saying, Bring back borders. That's what he kept ranting about, Lukas. Bring back the watchtowers and security lights and barbed wire and dogs and passport checks and people sent back to where they came from.

He asked her once more if she wanted to come over and join him. He said he had found the place with the tree, where they once stopped to sit in the rain together. She said she could not. She was busy getting ready for teaching.

Her voice was genuine, he would write. It was not mere politeness that made her ask him how he was doing. He said he was doing all right. Thanks, Katia. He said he'd had a minor scare out swimming. The tides can be very strong sometimes, he said, maybe it was a rip tide or something like that, where a river forms on the surface and flows against the waves, pulling the swimmer back out to sea. I found myself drifting across the bay onto the rocks. I'm fine, he said, totally fine, just a few cuts. I banged my knee against the rocks. That was a bit scary and I'm limping a bit but no harm done, I don't need crutches, put it that way.

I don't think I would make a surfer, he said. Then he laughed. There's a gang of surfers here, they want me to join them and get a board for myself. They go off chasing big waves all over the country, but it's not something I see myself getting into, not after this episode with the waves throwing me around like a piece of marine trash.

He was surprised that she was still listening. At one point, she was so silent that he thought she had been cut off, like she might have lost the signal in the café, or he had lost the signal out there along the coast, so he asked if she was still there and she said, Yes, I'm still here. He continued talking and said that while he got himself into difficulty, he had seen his father.

Where?

He was standing on the shore.

Your father?

Yes, he was standing on the strand waiting for me. He was the only person there, like he had come to make sure I got back to land safely.

Your father has been dead for years, Luki.

I know that, he said. I know he's dead, but he came back to talk to me. I know you think this is something I have invented in my journal, but it's true, Katia. You think I've gone nuts out here and maybe I have. You think I've started believing in ghosts, which is not like me at all, Katia. You know yourself, I have no time for the supernatural. Superstition. Even coincidences are just a matter of chance, like the odds of Emilia seeing that man in the furry pink jacket still alive today on the underground. My father, he said, might have been some kind of hologram. With the sun shining behind him on the shore, all I could make out was this dark shape of a man. I knew it was my father by his silent stare, like he was quietly asking what I was up to with my life. I know you think I'm imagining all of this, but does it really matter if he was real or not? He's been dead now for a long time and we still had this meeting on the strand. He must have pulled me out of the water while I was unconscious and then I woke up with him standing over me. Maybe I have become the illusion, he said, while she continued listening without a word. Maybe it's me that's invented. Me that's become a hologram.

Twenty-Six

He parked the car by the river and walked up through the town. He came to the clock tower and passed the shop with the toys and souvenirs on the corner. He came to the sports shop with all the rain macs and walking boots. The shop assistant showed him the same two surfboards on display at the back. He could not get himself to buy the one with the Aboriginal design, so he took the one with the image of a shark's teeth and one big shark eye. He carried the shark board along the street and was amazed, when he saw his own reflection passing by a shop window, how much he looked like a surfer. The board under his arm turned him into a man of extremes, willing to risk his life on gallant survival acts. Like he would soon be walking into pubs in bare feet and talking about nothing but the shape of waves and the experience of standing on the surf. Like he was already part of that community of surfers going on expeditions to find the most exciting waves around the world. He could see himself riding the curls, slipping through perfectly formed barrel waves until he disappeared. But there was something obviously false about all this. He was limping as he walked along the street with the surfing gear, so people could tell it didn't look right. A limping surfer drew their attention, covering up some injury with supremely athletic equipment.

He got back to the car and placed the newly bought surfboard in the boot after collapsing the back seats. He drove up to visit Brian and Gabi. When he arrived at the house, it was Brian who came out and stood at the door while Gabi remained just inside the hallway. The stairway behind her was covered in blue and gold light cast by the stained-glass window on the landing. He sat down and had a cup of tea with them and Gabi asked what had happened to his hand and why was he limping.

I was out swimming, he said. A rock came up and attacked me from underneath.

Brian laughed. Gabi didn't.

She knew by intuition that it was more than a swimming accident. Her therapeutic instincts assumed the worst. She waited for the full explanation and he merely said that he was not really suited to the water. He was never going to be a surfer. And the waves, he said, I can barely swim. He told them he had bought a surfboard but it was a bad idea. And now he was thinking that Omar would be more into something like that.

He's going back, Brian said.

This might change his mind.

I doubt it, Brian said.

His mind is fixed, Gabi said.

He told them that he had invited Mira to visit the island. He was hoping he could persuade Omar to come. Maybe if he got talking to the surfers and tried it out for himself, it might alter his opinion of the world, delay his decision. The surfers were like a family. A community of people that Omar could belong to. They travel like a bunch of nomads in search of magnificent waves all over the world.

His flight is booked, Gabi said.

He went out and opened the boot of the car. He took the surfboard out and limped over to the small cottage with the red door. He placed the surfboard up against the wall and knocked on the door. When Mira opened up, she was wearing white ear pods and took them out. She found him standing outside with the surfboard, like there was something out of character, the feel-good image didn't quite fit.

She laughed. Is that for me?

Well, actually, I was thinking of Omar.

She tilted her head with a questioning frown to indicate that it was a bit of a long shot. She knew her own son's mind. But you never knew, there might be something in it. She turned and called for Omar to come out.

Omar was wearing his hoodie and it immediately became clear that this was a mistake. The hoodie gave Omar an underground appearance, like he was more at home on the streets of some major city, shuffling along the pavement, not even taking his hands out of his pockets. How would he ever fit in with the positivity of surfers? His face, when it was possible to see him more clearly, bore a look of deep mistrust.

Have you ever tried surfing?

The question seemed utterly comical.

Omar just stared at him, then looked at the shark board leaning against the wall. The tag was still attached. The eye of the shark enlarged, with human eyelashes.

I bought it for myself, he said to Omar. But I can't use it right now because I got injured. Out swimming, I ran into the rocks. He showed the bandage on his hand and pointed at his knee. I gave myself a terrible bang on the knee, so I can't take up surfing for a while, at least.

Omar looked at his mother as though she was part of some conspiracy to prevent him from leaving.

You can borrow it, he said. Try it out. There's a bunch of guys on the island. They will lend you a wetsuit.

Omar looked as though he was being inducted into some religious cult.

You can swim, he said to Omar.

Omar didn't answer. Nor did Mira.

It's an amazing sport, so they tell me. I think you might love it, Omar. Something very special when you get lifted up by the wave.

Omar looked him in the eyes. Are you fucking joking?

There was a long silence while Omar was trying to gather his words. The offer of surfing was such an affront to their sorrow, he didn't even know where to begin.

Omar turned and went inside.

Mira glanced up with a half-smile and followed her son into the house.

He stood looking at the door. The surfboard was so out of place now, so inconsequential, so full of goodwill and apology, it began to dawn on him what a condescending miscalculation it was. How could he possibly have got it so wrong? His best intentions misguided to the point of insult.

Omar then came back out again. He had something to say. He raised his head up from under his hood and pointed at the surfboard. Are you taking the piss? Surfing.

It's good fun.

Good fun, Omar said. That's not going to bring them back. The women on that truck on their way home from work. You don't get it. You have no fucking idea, do you? You think you can just buy our grief. You think this will help our people. They need water and you come with a surfboard.

Omar closed the door.

The surfboard stood leaning against the wall with the teeth biting into the white plaster and the big shark eye looking at him with a mocking stare. Was it possible that the shark even winked at him? He felt like such a fraud carrying it back to the car. If there had been a dumpster to be seen, he would have thrown it straight in. He put the surfboard back into the boot and at least it was out of sight now. A hollow gesture of friendship that would solve nothing in the world. A hopeless bit of hope that convinced nobody, least of all himself.

Twenty-Seven

In his journal, he wrote this.

Surprised that Mira would still want to come. No more talk of surfing. Showed her some of the places I knew. Not the same as going back. More like seeing them for the first time. Like the landscape is altered by the person in your company. The fields were full of remorse.

She got into the car. She was wearing a grey jacket with a zigzag pattern. A light green T-shirt with the vague design of a carousel. Her hair was a deeper black than he had previously thought. Plaited behind with a tiny white ribbon.

He drove through the town, past the clock tower and the shop with the souvenirs and the shop where he had bought the surfboard. He thought of stopping to bring it back and get a refund, or maybe to exchange it for a good rain mac. He even thought of leaning the surfboard up against the shop window to get rid of the shame, but he continued driving and staring ahead without mentioning it again.

On the way out to the island, it was Mira who took the awkwardness out of the air by talking about a podcast she had been listening to, all about the intelligence of a giant octopus. Some of them have multiple brains and multiple hearts. They dance and talk to each other with shades of ink.

You probably know all this, she said.

No, I don't.

Humans of the sea, they call them. They're so smart, she said. This guy on the podcast was saying it was mad how they didn't evolve to take over the world like us.

They might have done a better job, he said.

She laughed.

They don't live very long, she said. Not enough time to pass their talents on to the next generation.

They drove with the holy mountain appearing behind them. He turned himself into a tour guide, asking her if she had ever been on the holy mountain. She said there were so many places she still had not managed to get to. He said he had been up there once but there was cloud over the mountain and he saw nothing.

And that's another thing, she said, while they were driving into the sunshine. The podcast I was listening to said that some day Artificial Intelligence will be looking at us like we're some giant squid who failed to evolve.

He was slow to reply and made a mental note in his head

to put in his journal that she smiled and leaned her elbow up against the window.

We'll be the squid of the earth, she said.

Squid of the future.

They came to a small town and stopped for coffee. Mira had a latte, and as she was taking the first sip, a fight broke out between two dogs. Everybody got up from their chairs. The café went into a state of emergency with lots of barking and growling and legs getting wound up in dog leads until the fighting dogs were separated and the woman who owned the smaller dog was furious. She called it the height of aggression and spoke directly to Mira as if it was her fault.

In the car afterwards, he said to Mira, Do you think Artificial Intelligence will evolve to get beyond racism?

She looked straight ahead as she spoke.

The bigger question is this. Will Artificial Intelligence be able to do all those human things that we do so well, like love and sorrow and loneliness? Will it speak from the heart? Will it be able to express how lucky we are to be alive?

The sun came out in strong flashes as they drove out to the island. The brightness was reflected on the surface of the road. The fields lit up like a pinball alley, yellow, brown and luminous green. And parallel to the road at one point, they saw a family of cyclists with their helmets on riding along a greenway. The greenway had initially been built as a railway line, back in the nineteenth century, so that fresh fish could be brought by train from the west coast to the fish markets of London. Now the trail looked like a moving belt. A family travelling backwards while they drove by on the road at a different level above them.

They crossed the bog with the windows open and got the smell of turf. The smoke was drifting out to sea in a blue haze. The firemen with their red tenders were hosing the ground and he told her what he had been told by the woman of the house, that a bog fire was a rabbit in a burrow with many corridors.

When they got to the place where the emigrant normally looks around to catch the last glimpse of the island, he slowed down and pointed at the view ahead. He told her what the woman of the house had told him about the people who left on the bus turning around to wave goodbye one last time before the island disappeared. They were travelling in the opposite direction, the non-leaving direction. As they drove past that point of last looking back, they could feel what it was like to catch the first sighting of home. Driving into a homecoming. That familiar glimpse of the mountains rising up in the distance to greet them. It must have felt to the returning emigrant like a huge shudder coming up through the suspension of the bus, right up through the seats, into the heart. A welcome in which the people of the island pushed the mountains up out of the earth to let them know that nothing has changed. A million years of geological formation rising up out of the landscape to let them know they have been waiting a million years for them to come back. The uplifting hearts. The faces and the smiles and the embracing, all the sadness of leaving reversed now.

The returning emigrant could hardly wait any longer to be among the people and the mountains and the first sight of the sea where you thought you might drive over the edge into the ocean. Here it was, the moment in which that last sighting of the mountains was turned around and the landscape was converted from fantasy to fact. With every second, every passing tree and stone wall, the furthest place in the world came closer and closer and closer. And then all the people embracing, the shyness, the misfitting words, the stories, the gifts brought home from another country, the time that was lost and the time regained, and the suitcase thrown out onto the sea.

Twenty-Eight

It was only to be expected that when he brought her to visit the deserted village it would remind her of home. The scattered ruins of an entire people who had been driven away from their homes by hunger with no sign of aid coming to rescue them. The abandoned houses now seemed even more hollow and empty than ever before. And as they walked through the rows of fallen walls, Mira said it made her think of the apartment block where she once lived with her family. She was told there was a phone ringing underneath the rubble for a couple of days and then the battery must have eventually run out.

It made me so angry, she said.

She stepped inside one of the low ruins and stood looking out through the window. It had no frame, just a stone opening where the occupants must have leaned out to see who was coming up from the coast. Where the mother, he imagined, might have passed a piece of bread out to one of her children or maybe where the cat used to lie on the ledge in the sun. Where you could see the ocean and the cliffs on the far side of the bay going red with the sun beginning to go down.

She said she had become attached to her anger. It was impossible to let it go or shut herself off from what had happened. She had a friend she was in touch with, a school friend who told her the story of the mobile phone ringing among the ruins. Her friend told her how lucky she was to have got away. It was hard to get clean water to drink. It was hard to wash. Her friend had been living in a camp and she had a small mirror but she stopped looking at herself because her face had become so thin.

The ruins they had come to visit seemed so far back in time now. It was an ancient emptiness. A piece of distant history. Where the pain and the sorrow of the people who once lived there had somehow dissipated over time, a suffering that was hard to witness because it was so long ago.

It made the catastrophe of her people even more vivid. She said that she had managed to escape with her son by paying bribes all the way. A journey out of Hell. All she could think of was getting her son to safety and she was willing to do anything to make that happen. She didn't want to go into all the scary things they faced along the way. It was not something you would want to remember, and she could rejoice at the fact that she had made it to this quiet place in the world.

She could never leave the anger behind. She was angry for all the people who didn't make it out. Her mother on the horse-drawn truck with the rubber wheels of a car. All of my mother's friends and companions coming home from work, she said. It feels like some kind of betrayal, not to be angry, like I was letting them all down by surviving and being safe.

She stood in the doorway of the cottage and he thought for a moment of the place where she came from being restored to what it was, the homes and schools and playgrounds and hospitals thriving as they once were. The traffic on the streets in motion and the truck with the women going by with their legs swinging over the side moving through the traffic.

It's Omar I'm worried about, she said. I have passed that anger on to him.

He listened.

He's full of rage now, she said. Full of resentful energy that he can do nothing about, apart from going back to join the fight. Like he needs to get even with history. Like you need a certain amount of anger and hatred to get justice. He doesn't have any friends, she said. He keeps to himself most of the time. He has not connected with anyone at work either, only with his people online. I've been trying to get him to take up some kind of sport, hurling or football, that would get him into the community. But he's made up his mind now. He won't rest until he goes back to stand up for his people.

She was silent for a while and there was nothing he could think of saying that didn't sound utterly out of place and full of hopeless good will. He had become a listener. That was what people needed most now. Listeners. There was a shortage of listeners worldwide. The world needed to recruit a couple of million listeners right away. Like there should be a place in every city and small town called the listening room, where people could go and tell their stories.

I used to think everything was against us, she said. All the ordinary things that didn't work out, like some application form. Some money that was meant to come. Even the weather seemed like an insult. Those terrible things in the past have become my story. It's our identity. I still want to cry every time I think of home. I can't even say the word without choking.

She stepped out of the stone ruin and stood looking across the sea.

It's beautiful here, she said.

She took in the wide view of the sea and the mountains all around her as though it was a fabrication that she could never quite believe.

My God, she said. It's so beautiful.

She was trying to stop worrying.

There is nothing I can do to stop Omar going back, she said. I did everything to get him here and it's a miracle that we made it. He knows all that. He knows the luck that was needed to make it out. But he has made up his mind, a calling in his head that he cannot shake off.

They were making their way back along the road with the stream passing along the side and no other noise apart from the sound of sheep on the hillside. The sea was a good distance away and silent. The surfers were out on the waves. Black shapes with the gift of walking on water.

She stopped before getting into the car and said that her father told her what it was like in prison. He was held in military detention without trial before he was eventually released. She said it was hard to keep in touch with him and she never knew if he was back in detention or not. Her father told her that while he was in prison one of the prisoners was given a choice to go home for a day. He was offered a once-in-a-lifetime opportunity to visit his family for twenty-four hours. Then he would be re-arrested and taken back to where he had been kept for many months, tied to one of the beds, soldiers banging on the steel frame whenever they fell asleep. The other prisoners kept telling him how lucky he was to be chosen in this mother of all lotteries. He was getting what they all dreamed of, every minute of the day. Even a brief glimpse of home and the faces of children, she said. Who wouldn't take up such an offer of freedom, even a short one? He would be mad to turn it down. But the prisoner who had been offered the golden choice eventually told the soldiers he didn't want to go home. It was just a further form of torture. The soldiers laughed and maybe that was the worst kind of humiliation, she said, the freedom of choice given and withdrawn again.

They got back into the car. The smoke had moved away to another part of the island and the view was clear out as far as the headlands. They could see the surfers now standing around on the shore as the day came to an end.

Thanks for trying to get him interested in something else apart from the suffering of his people, she said.

He didn't speak.

You can't change Omar. Surfing would take away his dignity, Lukas.

It was so thoughtless of me, he said.

His heart is with his people, she said. Those who are dead and those still living. Nothing will keep him from going back. It would be like some kind of surrender to happiness. We don't feel entitled to that kind of fun. It would be like the man in prison who was offered a day with his family, then having to go back and give himself up again.

He drove down to the coast and parked the car by the beach, not in the parking area outside the guesthouse but a bit further out along the shore. They walked out on the strand and she found a piece of driftwood that was shaped like a sword. She held it up to the sea and stuck it into the sand.

She took off her shoes and stepped into the water and said it was not all that cold. There was a moment in which he had to remind himself, when the light caught her in a silhouette, it was not Katia but Mira he was looking at. She had begun to claim a place in his memory, supplanting those moments he kept in his journal like a museum of ancient treasures. It was not exactly the same spot where he had once stood with Katia when the sun was going down, but close enough to feel like some re-enactment. Or maybe what was taking place was some erasure in which there was no returning, only going further and further away. All forward now to the outermost. The innermost outermost.

They stood for a moment side by side being looked at by the sea. Behind them along the road, they heard the motorbike going by and the couple seemed by now to have become invisible. It was just the sound of the engine going by that was left. The surfers were coming back along the strand carrying their shields under their arms.

Further along the strand in the other direction, they saw the old schoolteacher. The shore-ranger, he said. He goes around collecting all kinds of objects along the coast to bring home. He keeps them in a shed at the back of his house. Does he sell them, she asked, or what does he do with them? He told her that the man never showed them to anyone, he just keeps all that stuff he's been gathering for years like some kind of memory bank. A bit like people keep a journal, he said, to remember stuff they want to hold on to that might have gone missing.

Must start doing that, she said.

In the pub, they sat at the table with the map of the island behind them and had fish and chips. When the musicians got going, he drew Mira's attention to the woman playing the accordion with bright green fingernails on black buttons. Mira was sitting beside him, facing the musicians in her zigzag jacket, he would later write. Brown eyes and white teeth and black hair in a pub that had green fingernails on black buttons and black pints with white necks and the voices of people talking and the surfers sitting at another table in bare feet.

It was late by the time they left the pub. They walked down the path and there was no need to hold up his phone to light the way. The moon was hidden, but there was a brightness all around the fields. The sea was crashing on the shore as always. They got back to where he had parked overlooking the strand and he said he would drive her back to Westport, but they sat in the car without moving. There was something that needed to be said between them and he didn't want to drive away while the moon behind a thin cloud gave the surface of the sea a pale face. The windows were open on either side for a slight bit of air movement and the bedroom scent of seaweed in the car.

He turned to her and said it was maybe not the right place to say this with the moon out, but there was something he wanted her to know. It had to do with the photo of the women on the back of the truck that she had shown him on her phone. The idea of them all being killed by a single missile strike was on his mind all the time.

Here's the thing, he said, with his hands on the steering wheel as though they were driving across the ocean. And this is what I wanted to say to Omar, he said, but I just went about it in the wrong way. My father had a map of red dots on the wall of his office when I was a boy. The red dots, I found out later, marked the places where people had been buried in mass graves. My mother's people lie underground in one of those locations. She's not buried there, but my father used to bring us there to lay flowers after she died.

Twice, he and his brother were brought there, in May, but there was nothing to see apart from a steel gate into a field. It was only at that point, talking to Mira, that he understood how important those trips were. How much that place meant to them.

We tied the flowers to the gate.

She continued listening.

What I'm trying to say is this, he said.

Mira was looking at him while he was addressing the pale face of the sea in a slow voice.

It's impossible to compare grief. How would you measure something like that? Grief is too big, he said. It's like trying to measure infinity.

What he wanted to say to her and could not find the right words for and later clarified in his journal, was that the absence of people you love is beyond comparison. It was impossible to equate the grief of his people with the grief of her people. It's not some kind of numbers thing. There is no equality in suffering. Only duplication. Adding more red dots. More dead bodies. History on top of history. Emptiness upon emptiness.

They stared at the silver highway across the water. A single-lane track to the end of the earth. They were travelling on the road of collective sorrow. Two people coming together in a shared sense of loss that came closer to love.

I guess I'm trying to stop the red dots reappearing, he said. The red dots in your country adding to the red dots on my father's map.

She placed her hand on his arm.

That's all I want, he said. I want to stop the red dots spreading to other parts of the world.

I will tell Omar, she said.

She left her hand on his arm and they carried on staring at the sea. The air across their faces was full of glitter. The stars were busy. The night was warm and the sound of the surf was coming in slow, sweeping strokes of long black hair being softly brushed in front of a mirror before sleep.

Here's an idea, he then said, when it was already past midnight and it seemed a bit late at that point to be driving all the way back across the bog with the yellow signs warning drivers not to go over the edge.

Why don't you stay at the guesthouse? he said. I'll sleep in the car. It's so warm tonight.

I couldn't do that, she said.

Seriously, he said. You're very welcome. You'll have the place to yourself.

Are you sure?

Absolutely. I will explain it to the woman of the house, then drive you back tomorrow.

The woman of the house still had her light on as always. He closed the front door, and as they stood for a moment in the hallway in front of the portrait of the writer with the black beret, she wanted to know who it was.

Who is that?

It's a German writer who stayed here once, he said. Way back in the last century. He had the scar of war on his forehead, maybe that's why he wore the beret and possibly didn't even take it off at night in bed.

He led her down the hallway to his room. The bed was made as always. The towels neatly stacked beside the sign that said, Please don't take towels to the beach. He left the key in the door and assured her it was no problem at all, he would explain everything to the woman of the house in the morning. He was seen leaving again, closing the front door quietly to keep the sand out, knowing that the writer from the last century would tell the woman of the house it was too late to drive back to Westport and he was happy to stay in the car with his journal.

Twenty-Nine

He was in early, sitting at the same breakfast table as always. His journal lay open on the table while he was staring out the window, trying to remember all the things the sea had been telling him during the night – stories of boatmen out fishing for turbot with long lines and torches, patches of the water that were calm while other patches were rough, the cliff lighthouse on a nearby island shining in rotation across the water, ships that delivered parcels of cocaine, one of which was found on the shore one morning and brought home by the shore-ranger to be kept unopened in his shed, stories of the deep and stories of lovers who slept on the beach, just beyond reach of the waves.

He was trying to figure out what exactly he was going to say to the woman of the house when she came marching into the room with a frown on her face.

What kind of woman of the house do you take me for?

He put up his hands, ready to explain.

She stood in front of him with her arms folded. She knew perfectly well there was some information being withheld. He had no explanation.

Why didn't you tell me?

I was just about to tell you, he said.

If only you told me she was coming, she said, I would have put fresh sheets on the bed. New pillow cases. I would have put flowers in the room. I would have left a tray with a scone and some jam. And a bottle of complimentary water.

And what are you doing sitting there at the single table with your journal, writing down God knows what little secretive thoughts you have in your head in a language that I can't read anyway? Move over here, she said, where the table is laid for you both, for God's sake.

He gathered up his journal and his pen like a delinquent student and moved to the other table, about to explain the whole story to her with his utmost honesty, but she would not allow him to speak.

Let her sleep, she said. She got in so late, my God, you're such a buttoned-up man, Lukas. What am I going to do with you at all? Did nobody teach you to leave a note?

She turned and went out to the kitchen. Then she came back in again moments later, her head in the door at an angle and her hand on the frame.

What's her name?

His mind went blank.

Your guest, Lukas.

Mira, he said, after another moment of hesitation.

She smiled and disappeared.

The writer with the black beret in the hallway by the front door would have told her it was not his wife but a woman from the century of refugees.

When Mira came into the breakfast room in her zigzag jacket, the woman of the house came rushing back to ask if she would prefer tea or coffee. It was Mira's shoulder that the woman of the house left her hand on this time, asking what cereal she might like and what lovely black hair she had. No hair colouring could ever be that black, look at me, she said, laughing, going all grey now the colour of stone walls. Her hair used to be black, she said. People would say she was a true Celt and there was a hairdresser in Westport who promised to dye her hair the blackest colour in the entire catalogue, but what was the point? It would never be what it was once, so why keep trying?

Over breakfast, he asked Mira to write a note in his journal. It was not something he had ever asked anyone to do before. He opened the journal on a blank page and put in the date, along with the name of the guesthouse and the part of Ireland they were in. He gave her the pen and she took a moment to reflect, then wrote in lovely oval handwriting.

Thanks for taking me to the lost village. Feels like you brought me home.

X Mira

They took their time over breakfast and sat at the table for a while longer, watching the surfers walking down to the shore with their black gear on and the boards under their arms. Then he said he wanted to show her the bog. The silence up there was like no place on earth, just a hint of a breeze like the sound of an accordion on the wind.

On the way out, they passed the portrait of the German writer once more, standing with the cigarette in his mouth on one of the empty roads. She wanted to know more about him and he told her that the writer had come to the island after the Second World War to find some peace of mind.

Did he find it?

No, he said. I think the tranquillity of this place only made him more anxious to go back and change his own country. The silence here made him confront the silence in his own people. The crimes that went unspoken. He was like a stranger at home. He used to say that nowhere in the world could you feel so estranged as you did in your own country. Sometimes you can't even recognise your hand.

The writer, he told her, was said to have too much empathy. Maybe it was the cruelty he had witnessed during the war that made his heart go out to other people. There's a German word for it – *Mitleid*. It described the concept of co-suffering. When a person feels the pain of others. The writer with the black beret answered the call of human co-suffering at the expense of his own art. It once led him into a daring act of rescue. He had a secret chamber built into the back of his car so that he could smuggle a famous pianist across the Iron Curtain out of Czechoslovakia. People-smuggling is what they would call it now, only the writer was not doing it for money. In fact, he was risking his life and his family on this dangerous mission to rescue the pianist from the Soviet Union and bring her to safety in the West.

The pianist was a small woman, he told her. She must have nearly lost her mind when they were crossing the border. No windows. Just two small air vents. It must have felt like a travelling coffin, hardly able to breathe and terrified of coughing, with the border guard checking in behind the seat. It was a miracle she was not detected.

He made a note in his head to write in his journal as soon as he got a chance.

Novelist. Human-trafficking.

He said the woman of the house had told him that her mother remembered the writer arriving in that car like it was a spacecraft, floating along the roads with no wheels. The writer crashed the car one day and it was abandoned after that. Used to keep chickens for a while before it went for scrap along with the fugitive chamber that nobody knew about.

The insurrectionist writer whose books were once read by everyone across the world and for which he was awarded the Nobel Prize, once declared that it was the duty of a writer to intervene, to be involved, to go too far. The outlaw writer, corrupted by his own conscience. Crossing the line between fiction and reality like a protagonist in his own novels, turning himself into a reckless piece of human art.

That writer, he said, as they were getting into the car and the woman of the house waved at them from the door, used to talk about history like he was pulling his own teeth. If he was alive today, he said, that twentieth-century writer would be pulling whatever teeth he had left over what was happening right now.

They felt the bounce of peat under their feet. The smoke was being carried away to the other side of the island. The sun was out strong and they saw a horse standing on the path, grazing on bits of new grass along the verge.

It was the grey horse from the grey field. In the distance, they could see a man and a boy. He waved and the boy waved back. The horse reared its head up and snorted. But then, as Mira came close, the horse remained utterly calm, with no sense of alarm or suspicion. No fear of the bog fire underground.

Perhaps the horse knew the rain was coming.

She touched the horse's neck with the flat of her hand. Running it underneath and gently holding the horse's head with both hands, face to face, forehead to forehead, speaking in her own language.

He told her about the event with the horse being injured on the road and running into the sea and the boy swimming after it. How the boy was rescued and the surfers got hold of the leather reins floating free on the top of the water and brought the horse back to the strand.

She examined the scar with her fingers, and even then, the horse remained calm, as though it had no memory of being afraid. He was expecting the horse to remember what was so frightening. The hidden facts in the back room of his mind, all those fucked-up things he carried with him. The alarming piece of history that burned underneath his conscious memory.

It was no longer the horse in the war painting with its head thrown back and a tongue raging out through crooked teeth like a screaming spear. Not the horse with tiny eyes and spiked-up ears and nostrils flaring in terror. Not the horse of human massacre and murder and re-murdered people left in unknown graves, but the serene grey horse on a serene blanket bog with the squeaking of larks in the air.

He stepped forward and allowed himself to put his hand on the horse's neck. The horse felt safe and did not suddenly bolt at the sign of danger. There was a calmness in the horse that matched the calmness of his own mind now. The horse's head was moving up and down in a gesture of acknowledgement. The grey mane fell in curls and the tail was sweeping in a gentle rhythm from side to side. And that one big horse-aware eye, looking down with horse trusting, horse certain, horse-in-a-timeless-bog-with-no-need-to-be-afraid horse.

A light rain had begun to fall. The world was a room. A silent room, sectioned off by the sea on one side and the mountains on the other and a couple of trees curled inland by winter winds. The rain could hardly be called rain. More like a set of net curtains hanging over the landscape. They looked back to see the horse standing in the middle of the room now with one of its hind legs casually limp, staring inland and blinking from time to time with the water collecting on its eyelashes. A solitary grey horse, held in a trance by the stillness, as though it had been there since the dawn of time.

Thirty

He parked on the hill. He was bringing them to the station, but there was plenty of time before the train left, so he asked Mira and Omar if he could take a photo of them sitting on the crooked bench. It looked like an exaggerated gesture of affection between a mother and son. Omar squashed at the lower end and his mother next to him as though they had both gone sliding down the incline and come to a stop at the steel armrest, Mira laughing and Omar staring ahead with his hood over his head, sitting at a seasick angle, his rucksack by his feet.

They walked down the hill together, all three of them. They came to the yellow pub and once again he forgot to look up to see the name, so it remained the yellow pub with some musical instruments in the window and a poster that said, Music tonight. Mira went inside to speak to the owner and he asked Omar to come with him, there was something he wanted to give him for the journey.

What?

It will fit into your bag, easily, he said.

Omar shrugged and threw his rucksack over his shoulder. They continued walking down the hill to the square with the clock tower. They crossed the street and came to the corner shop with the toys and souvenirs. A plastic fire engine. A couple of toy shovels. And toy sweeping brushes. And a basket full of footballs. There was a man with a peaked cap leaning in the doorway and it was hard to say if he was the owner or just somebody taking a break, waiting to get into a conversation with somebody passing by. A woman with a small boy was trying out one of the plastic lawnmowers and he overheard the man in the doorway saying to her that it was good the grass hadn't grown too long with the dry spell. There was a plastic poncho on a hanger swinging in the doorway as if to remind people passing by that, even if it hadn't rained in weeks, they might soon need a plastic poncho at the last minute.

He was limping as they went past the souvenir shop, Omar beside him with his hood down over his head. They passed the sports shop where he had bought the surfboard. They continued past the hardware shop with rolled-up sections of lino outside and he remembered Brian telling him that every house in the West of Ireland once had the same linoleum design in burgundy put down in the kitchen on the stone floor. And as they walked in silence, he lost track of time and turned into his own father.

Himself and Omar turned into his father and himself. The same determined stride along the street with neither of them asking or explaining where they were going.

They stopped at a bookshop. He brought Omar to the back of the store where they had a small display of notebooks and journals. He pointed to the different makes in different colours. Some lined and some blank. He told Omar that whenever he was buying a new journal for himself, even if it was the same make as the one he had had before, and sometimes he could only order them online from Paris, the first thing he did was to open up the journal in the middle somewhere and sniff the interior. It was, he said to Omar, like an open space, like breathing in a landscape going into infinity. Inhaling the blank pages made him think he could go anywhere in the world.

It gives me this great freedom. He told Omar that a new journal was like getting into a car and driving into the unknown. A journey you can take across the world without moving. You never know where the thing you write might take you.

Like what?

Anything you can think of, he said to Omar.

Omar said he had nothing to write.

You could write about the women on the truck, he said.

Omar raised his head under the hood, his eyes full of accusation.

The women?

It's a suggestion, he said. Just an example of the kind of thing you could put in a journal. The women as they appear in the photograph on your mother's phone. Left to right. Keep them recorded.

Keep them, how?

Their names.

The names, what good is that?

Your mother knows all their names, doesn't she?

That's not going to put things right.

You might be the only person who has their names documented, he said to Omar, all of them together, the order in which they appeared on the back of the truck coming home from work.

Before they were taken out.

Yes, he said. Before they were taken out.

A bomb that was made in your country, Omar said.

I wish I knew how to stop this, he said. Omar, it's not possible to undo these things, and that's why it's so important to write it down. It might not get justice for them. But it will stop the silence if you keep their names.

There was nothing left of them, Omar said. They could not be identified. No funeral. No graves. No headstones. My grandmother was among them and so was my aunt.

They loved playing cards. They were good at cards. And my cousin, she used to cheat, they called her the card shark. They just vanished. There is no place to bring flowers. Just that photograph my mother keeps on her phone. Nothing else.

Let the journal be their burial ground, he said to Omar. You can give them a proper resting place. Their headstones in writing, with their names and their dates of birth. As long as their names are written down, it will stop them disappearing. They won't stop being dead, but they will continue to exist as long as their names are not forgotten.

Omar said nothing more, just picked up one of the journals on display. He went for the navy cover and released the strap that kept it closed. He opened it out and put his face up to the pages and inhaled the emptiness inside. The unwritten emptiness. Full of content that had not yet been thought of. The unknown future. The unspoken past. Like undiscovered continents. Like going back to a time before time. Omar took in the sweet scent of paper. The trees it was made from. The forests and the saw mills. The machines that printed the lines. The guillotine that cut the pages and the glue that held the spine together.

Omar kept his face hidden in the new pages, inhaling the rich scent of unused paper. Perhaps he was concealing his grief in that moment by hiding his face. He didn't want to be seen with tears in his eyes. He was using the unused journal for a handkerchief, already staining the pages with his wounded mind. When he lifted his head up, there was a fragile hint of acceptance in his eyes before he turned his head down again.

They went to the till together. He invited Omar to pick a pen from a selection of pens on a rotating display. There was a pad underneath where customers had tested out the pens and made a few squiggles in varied thickness and somebody had written the word house three times in different pens including a red one. Another buyer had made a Celtic spiral in black. Omar picked one with blue ink and tried it out by drawing a small arrow with fins. As he paid for the journal and the pen with his credit card, he told Omar it was his private space, where he could be alone with nobody telling him what to do or what to think, a place to put down his ideas and his thoughts. Wherever he went in the world, this journal would be his best friend. Omar wrote his full name on the inside flap, then clamped the pen inside and closed over the strap that kept it shut. He put the journal into his black bag and they walked out into the street again.

They made their way past the clock tower and up the hill past the yellow pub to the car. Mira was waiting. They drove to the station. They stepped out and he shook hands with Omar, then watched him disappearing into the station with his mother. They didn't turn around, just walked inside, her hand on her son's shoulder. And while he was waiting for her to say goodbye to Omar on the platform, he sent her the photo of them both on the crooked bench together.

On the way back to the island, he passed the place of last looking back and saw the motorbike parked by the side of the road a little further on. There was no sight of the German couple and maybe, he thought, they were out walking on the bog and the woman's chronic pain had been healed. Maybe all that travelling up and down the island on the motorbike had finally massaged the nerves that were trapped and allowed her to walk free again.

He carried on driving and stopped once more at the field with the black and white cows. They were gone. The cows had done their day's work and the field was empty apart from some barn swallows flying low, circling around and creating an optical illusion. Their last chance for insects before the rain. The air still with anticipation. Nothing in the field but distance. Started with isolated drops, he wrote, single notes tapping on the roof. Sat staring at the tree, a copper beech, with moss around the base and roots like fat snakes disappearing into the earth. People will be happy now, he wrote. The bog fire has nowhere to hide. Rain drumming hard. Drumming with great feeling. Drumming a million hands on the roof.

Thirty-One

He stood on the shore looking out across the ocean. The sea was noisy. The waves were capped with white heads of foam. Gulls hovering like kites. A fine spray of sea water left a film of salt on his face, he could taste it on his lips. The autumn storms had come and the strand was dressed in a black fringe of seaweed. The surfers were gone. They had moved on to bigger waves elsewhere. There was nobody left now but himself and he told the sea what he had already told the woman of the house, even as the wind forced the words back into his mouth, that it was time for him to leave.

Where?

Berlin.

So, it's back home, then?

That's all I can do now, he said. Go back to Berlin and stop the silence.

He took the journal from his pocket and held it in his

hand. He flicked through the pages and they were nearly all used up. There was nothing he needed to add now at the last minute only one small note to confirm that he was leaving. He left the pen inside and replaced the rubber band that kept it closed. He put the journal up to his face and kissed the cover. Then he stood back and took aim and swung his arm and threw the journal onto the waves, like the custom of the returning emigrant, throwing the suitcase out to prove that he was home.

He gave out a great roar.

The journal sailed through the air and landed between two waves. It disappeared and came back and disappeared and came back into view again, a flat, orange-coloured object, rocking on top of the water. His travelling companion. His suitcase. His life refracted through words. The bashed-up story of his journey held afloat for a while and a gull coming to have a look. There was no need for him to keep that journal. No need to read over what he had written. Once the journal was consigned to the sea, entrusted to a safe place, he was released from the duty of keeping everything stored. Released from the duty of comparing the past with the present. That faculty for seeing the grand continuum of time as a gold-framed mirror in which the past is re-enacted into the future.

He watched the journal floating on the surface until it sank out of view, his life in living ink, the pages dissolving in salt, all those words going down into the deep like some great vault of memory below the sea.

The sea was getting ready for another storm. It was coming in from the Atlantic without much notice. A storm that had not yet been given a name on the weather channels. A storm that would live up to its name and lift pieces of farming equipment and take gates off hinges and throw anything around that was not fixed down. High winds that would lean on windows and a shoulder pushing the door. Delivering belongings to the far side of the island to be found and brought back to their owners. Winds that would drive a credit card into the side of a tree like a knife. Rain that would turn roads into rivers. A storm that would lift the sand and dump it in places where there had been no sand before. Freak weather conditions that would make people talk about something unnatural going on that was never there in living memory. Like the landscape could no longer be trusted and you had no idea what the temperature might be from day to day and the sea had never been as high before. The woman of the house would be calling it a visiting beach and her husband would be out with his bucket and spade returning the beach to the beach like he was digging out an ancient people from under layers of time.

Let the deep remain the deepest deep. Let the boulders from the deep continue coming up rounded off with age, like stone seals arriving on the shore. Let the sun keep sinking at the end of the day and turn the rocks into copper faces with eyes watching. Let the waves keep returning the words in the shape of sand.

The sea spoke with the sound of ages. What else was there left now but to keep rolling the waves? The sea would continue being the sea as it has been doing since the beginning of time and would be doing for the rest of eternity, waiting for him to come back soon.

Acknowledgements

Many thanks to Ciara Considine for her inspired literary instincts. Hans-Henner Becker for his huge historical insight. Special thanks to my agent Peter Straus. Also to Stephen Edwards at Rogers, Coleridge and White. Thanks also to Stephen Riordan and everyone at Hachette Books Ireland, John McHugh, Edward King, Gisela Holfter, Hans Christian Oeser, Deborah Byrne, Gráinne McGregor and Kevin Hartnett. The Arts Council in Dublin. Nora Gombringer and the Bavarian ministry for culture for their hospitality at Villa Concordia in Bamberg. And Bob Dylan, for that powerful line about this not being the time for our tears.